Amigas

A Formal Affair

Amigas

A Formal Affair

by Veronica Chambers

Created by Jane Startz
Inspired by Jennifer Lopez

Hyperion
New York

Printed in the United States of America
First Edition
1 3 5 7 9 10 8 6 4 2

J689-1817-1-11060

ISBN 978-1-4231-2366-8

Designed by Tyler Nevins

Visit www.hyperionteens.com

For my awesome sobrinas,
Magdalena and Sophia. Abrazos,
—V.C.

To my sweetest friends and loved ones,
Peter, Jesse, Kate, and Zoë.
Thanks for bringing me so much joy.
—J.S.

CHAPTER 1

IT WAS A PERFECT October day in southern Miami. Cool and just breezy enough for the palm trees to sway, but still early enough in the season that the rains hadn't begun yet. Carmen Ramirez-Ruben walked down the hall of her school, Coral Gables High. At her left was her best friend in the entire world, Alicia Cruz, and at her right was her second bestie, Jamie Sosa.

One of the coolest things about living in Miami was the diversity of its people. This mix of peoples and cultures was truly reflected at C. G. High, where you really couldn't judge a book by its cover. There were Indian students who were of Arab descent and Pakistanis who were Hindu. Black students might be Latinos from the Dominican Republic and Panama, or African Americans, or Jamaicans or Saint Lucians. A blond, blue-eyed girl might be from Venezuela, and a dark-haired girl with olive skin might be from Kansas.

All this diversity didn't mean that there weren't cliques—the worst of which was the SoBees. They called themselves that because they planned all of the school's socials and benefits. Like the partners of Amigas Inc., the SoBees were a multicultural and multi-talented crew. But unlike the *amigas*—who, though well liked by their fellow students, were not interested in being part of the superpopular C.G. power elite—the SoBees were zealously dedicated to maintaining their elevated social status.

One member, Maya Clark-Hayward, was a tall, thin African American girl with café au lait skin and thick curly hair that looked like something out of a shampoo commercial. Her mother owned a string of radio stations nationwide, and the inside of Maya's locker was covered with photos of her and the singers and stars whom she had met when they stopped by the locally owned station to do promotions.

Another SoBee, April Yunayama, was Japanese American, and third-generation Miami elite. A collector of designer clothes, she was petite in stature and rail thin. April also loved to discuss people's looks and would ask her two BFF SoBees over and over, on a daily basis, whether the outfit she was wearing made her look fat.

And the third SoBee, Dorinda Carrassquillo, was a Dominican, who was notorious for being the most sarcastic person at C. G. High—and the unofficial head of the group. Her father owned several luxury-car dealerships all over the city. Though she only had a learner's permit, Dorinda had received a car—a Kelly green Escalade—for her *quinceañera*. And because she was too young to drive without an adult with a driver's license accompanying her, the family's maid, Jacinta, was forced to ride along with the SoBees everywhere they wanted to go.

As the three *amigas* neared their classroom, the SoBees were putting up posters for the winter formal. "*Hola, chicas,*" Dorinda said, handing the *amigas* a snowflake-shaped Save the Date card. "This is going to be the best winter formal ever. You all will probably learn a thing or two for your little party-planning business."

At the words *little* and *party-planning*, Jamie lurched forward ever so slightly. Carmen put a calming hand on her shoulder and subtly shook her head. Now was not the time or place.

"Thanks," Alicia said, taking the card. Smiling, she began walking toward the classroom again, her friends close behind.

The SoBees were safely out of earshot when Jamie went ahead and let her Bronx show. "Amigas Inc. is *huge*. It's no 'little party-planning business.' Girls like her work my last nerve!"

"Forget about it," Alicia laughed. "They're just jealous. This is going to be our first school formal and I'm totally psyched. Even the SoBees can't ruin that for me."

"I agree," Carmen said. "And of course they're jealous. All they know how to do is spend their parents' money to make an event fabulous. They don't worry about budgets or making sure *other* people are happy." She cast a disapproving eye as the SoBees teetered away in their five-inch gladiator heels. "We have a *real* company. Our *quinces* are off the hook, and we make all our own loot."

The summer before, the three girls, joined by Alicia's then close friend—and now boyfriend—Gaspar (Gaz) Colón, had formed their own business, Amigas Incorporated. In what seemed like no time at all, they had become one of the most popular *quinceañera* (Sweet Fifteen) planners in the city—and beyond. Recently, Gaz had decided to quit the business to concentrate on his music, but he still provided playlists and performed at all of Amigas Incorporated's gigs. In an ironic twist, since leaving, Gaz's romance with Alicia had really bloomed; in large part it was because they no longer had to deal with the added tension of having to work together.

As Latinas, Alicia, Carmen, and Jamie knew first-hand just how important a *quince* was, not only to the girl who was turning fifteen, but to her entire family. Traditionally, a *quinceañera* marked a Latina's transition from child to woman, and the ceremony, which started at the church and often culminated in a huge party that lasted until the early hours of the morning, could be as big an event as a wedding. Some parents started saving for a girl's *quince* from the moment she was born. Amigas Inc. had planned *quinces* that ranged in budget from $1,000 to $25,000. It was pretty heady stuff for three girls who themselves had all just turned fifteen in the last year. But they had never backed down from a challenge. Ever! When they got together, there wasn't anything they couldn't do. Each girl brought with her to the business a rich cultural heritage and a unique talent.

While the three *amigas* had worked hard over the last year, that didn't mean they hadn't played hard, too. Every chance they got, they took off for the beach, hung out at Alicia's house, or checked out one of their favorite hotel pools.

And then there was the dating. That had to be fit in between school, the job, and friend time. But they made it work. Alicia and Gaz were going strong and were the longest lasting couple of the group.

Even the impossible-to-please Jamie was hooked up with someone. Amigas Inc.'s resident artist had grown up in the South Bronx, or the boogie-down, as she liked to call it. A dark-skinned Latina whose family came from the Dominican Republic, she had a blunt and sometimes brutal take on things, which she called "keeping it real." Amazing though it seemed, Jamie was still dating Dash Mortimer, the salsa-dancing, Spanish-speaking, top-ranked teen golf star she had met when Amigas Inc. had been hired to plan a *quince* for his sister, Bianca. Although Jamie was loath to admit it, it had pretty much been love at first sight for both of them, and they had been nearly inseparable ever since.

And then there were Carmen and Domingo. The gorgeous computer nerd–über hottie and Carmen were practically attached at the hip. Domingo had become a fixture at her house; the couple spent hours together, and when they couldn't see each other, Domingo would send Carmen little love texts to let her know he was thinking about her. It seemed picture perfect.

But at that moment, standing in the hall, when

Carmen knew she should have been smiling and laughing and planning for the big dance, she wasn't. Her smile seemed frozen, forced.

Because she and Domingo were over. And she had no date for the dance. And even though she would never have dared admit it out loud, thinking about Domingo still hurt . . . a lot.

CHAPTER 2

IT HAD BEEN two months now, but Carmen still couldn't believe that she and Domingo were done. And the worst part was, she had been the one to initiate it.

Domingo had been a *chambelán*—sort of like a knight, without the shining armor—at Carmen's *quinceañera*, a Lati-Jew-na affair that Amigas Inc. had planned to reflect all the different elements of her background. Domingo had also been the first boy that she'd kissed, the first boy that she'd ever taken home to meet her parents, and the first boy who had motivated her parents to call out, "Leave the door open," whenever the couple went upstairs to her room.

Then Domingo had gotten into his dream school: Savannah College of Art and Design. In Georgia. A full 485 miles away. He planned to study interactive media and video-game design. Although he hadn't chosen it because of her, it was also a school with an excellent program in fashion, and Carmen was a gifted designer. She sewed all of her own clothes, and everything she wore looked as though it had come straight from some major couture house. If in two years, when Carmen was ready for college, they were still together, it might be nice if they were to go to the same school. That was what they told each other: *It might be nice.* No pressure. No heavy-duty plans. Just an open door that beckoned with possibility.

At the beginning of the summer, before Domingo left for college, they had sat side by side on Carmen's bed, cell phones in hand, open to their calendars. They had mapped out trips that would lessen the amount of time they'd be separated from one another. He would come back to Miami for a weekend at the end of September, so they'd never spend more than twenty-one days apart. Carmen's mother, under the impression that they'd be starting college visits early, had agreed to take Carmen to Savannah for a weekend in late October or early November. Domingo would be back for Thanksgiving, and after that it was a short sixteen-day sprint until he was home for Christmas break. It was going to be so simple, really. They'd concentrate on work when they were apart. They would focus only on each other when they were together. And thank God for Skype and free rollover cell-phone minutes. They would make it. They had to. . . . Things were so good between them.

Together, they could spend hours, working side by side, speaking in a kind of abbreviated sign language. Domingo would tap away at his computer. Carmen would jump from her sketchbook to her sewing machine. Every once in a while, they stopped to show each other something. One or the other would nod, offer a suggestion, walk over, and plant a kiss on their beloved's lips. But mostly, there was this beautiful silence. The hum of two people who needed few words to communicate what was in their hearts.

Which was why, a few weeks before Domingo was scheduled to head to Georgia, Carmen started to have a sickening feeling in the pit of her stomach. She'd begun to feel that, as much as she loved Domingo, they were Alicia and Gaz in reverse. Alicia and Gaz had first spent years as best friends, with a frisson of tension underneath the surface, but never enough to spark anything real—until finally, they got it together and started dating. Carmen feared that she and Domingo were the exact opposite: all sparks at the start, but, with the increased distance between them, bound to fall into the just-friends category, until there was nothing but the memory of romance.

Because she'd sensed it, because she'd spent so many quiet hours with Domingo, she wasn't surprised when he rang the doorbell unexpectedly one hot August afternoon. It was as though she had willed him to come over. And the look on his face didn't surprise her, either. It mirrored her own—a desire to be together forever, mingled with the realization that they needed to break up.

"Go on a boat ride with me?" Domingo asked. He handed her a hastily wrapped bouquet of wildflowers that looked as though he might have picked them himself. They were her favorite kind.

"Of course," she answered as she took the flowers into the kitchen and looked for just the right unfussy vase to put them in. Settling on a butter yellow ceramic pitcher, she put the flowers into water and grabbed her keys as she walked out the door.

In the boat, Domingo rowed, as he usually did. She liked to watch him, marveling at how his light brown arms moved with such graceful precision. On especially hot days, like this one, she could see his sunglasses begin to steam up. She wanted to be patient, to let him be the one to raise the topic of separating, of them each beginning school with a completely fresh start. But she couldn't help herself. In the Ramirez-Ruben household, you spoke early if you wanted to be heard.

"I don't want to break up, but I think we should break up," she whispered, staring down at the bottom of the boat.

"But I don't want to date other people," Domingo mumbled, looking away from her.

"Me, neither," Carmen added. "But I don't think this is about other people. I want this to end when we're still happy with one another. Instead of waiting until you feel like it is a burden to come see me, or that it takes you away from the life you should be leading with all your heart and soul, almost five hundred miles away."

"*Mi amor*, let's not say the words," Domingo implored her. "Let's not use the words *break up* or *ending* or *done* or *finished*. Not now. Not yet."

Carmen leaned across the little turquoise rowboat and put both of her hands on his. "Is *I will always love you* okay?"

Domingo nodded and kissed her.

Carmen pulled away and looked at him now, not afraid anymore, not wanting to look anywhere else.

"Is *I'll miss you* okay?" she asked.

"I think it is," Domingo replied. But this time when he kissed her, she could feel his tears wet her cheek, taste them salty against his skin.

Then he did something unexpected. He laughed. "We're too mature," Domingo said, quickly wiping the tears from his face. "I mean, look at us. We're sitting here being all cool. Why aren't you screaming?"

"I know what you mean," she agreed. "We should drag this out. Have a big nasty fight around Thanksgiving . . ."

"We could make up around December twelfth, after I take my last final," Domingo continued, playfully.

Carmen laughed then, too. "But the thing to do would be to totally ruin Christmas. We'd have to break up again. And out of decency, we'd both have to spend the entire Christmas and New Year's in mourning. Which would suck."

Domingo began to row the little boat back to the Ramirez-Ruben family dock. "If we break up now," he wondered aloud, "would I be over you by Christmas?"

Carmen raised an eyebrow. "Possibly. But remember, we weren't going to use the words *break up*."

"So what do you suggest?" Domingo asked, as he tied the rowboat to the little dock and helped Carmen onto the shore.

Carmen smiled, held his hand, then kissed him with all the wild abandon of a *telenovela* star. "We've got six days before you leave for college. Let's see how many different ways we can come up with to say, 'I love you.'"

Domingo placed his hands over his heart, then pointed at Carmen and smiled.

"What's that?" Carmen asked curiously.

"It's sign language for *I love you*," Domingo replied, slinging an arm around Carmen's shoulder as they walked back into the Ramirez-Ruben home. "There's a busboy at Bongos who's hearing-impaired. He's been teaching a bunch of us at the restaurant how to sign."

"Let me see that again," Carmen asked coyly, as they stood at her front door.

Domingo repeated the gesture.

Carmen shook her head. "I don't think that means *I love you*."

"Really?" Domingo asked, his eyes widening. "I didn't know you signed. What does it mean?"

"It means *please don't put so much starch in my shirt*," Carmen said, before collapsing in giggles.

Domingo smiled. "Very funny, *loca*. How will I ever find anyone who makes me laugh the way you do?"

As Carmen took her keys out of her pocket and

opened the door to her home, she wanted to say, "You *won't* find anyone who makes you laugh as much as I do." She wanted to add, "*Please* don't find anyone." She looked at Domingo, and right away she could tell that he knew just what she was thinking. She leaned in to kiss him, and this time it was her own tears that wet her cheeks.

It might have been because neither of her best friends had been through the breakup of their first loves, or it might have just been too painful, but Carmen didn't want to talk about Domingo or the twinge she felt whenever he crossed her mind when she was out with the girls. By the time school started in September, she was managing to think about him only roughly fifteen times a day. While not great, it was a heck of a lot better than the fifty or more times per day she had thought about him when they first "broke up." Now that it was the beginning of October and the *amigas* were already a month into their junior year of high school, she thought of him only four or five times a day. By Thanksgiving, she reasoned, he'd be a once-a-day memory. And by Christmas, she'd be over him. At least, that's what Carmen told herself. So she kept her still healing heart out of the conversations with her *mejores amigas*.

But that didn't mean her best friends didn't worry. Or try to get her to talk. Before school started, Alicia and Jamie had fretted obsessively about Carmen— calling her every day to see if she were lonely or needed a cheer-up trip to the beach or mall. And while Carmen had appreciated the way they dragged her on cheesy, touristy glass-bottom boat rides and plied her with pints of *dulce de leche* ice cream, Carmen *never* talked about the breakup. She insisted over and over again that she really was fine. And so, as time passed, her friends began to believe that she was telling them the truth. . . .

CHAPTER 3

NOW, A FEW months later, Carmen shook off her old memories and leaned against a locker. She looked at the Save the Date card for the winter formal as she half listened to Alicia go on about the SoBees. "You know, they're obnoxious. *Es la verdad.* But even so, I'm pumped. We're juniors now, upperclassmen. We can go to winter formal. It will be like a practice run for prom."

Jamie tried to hold out and hide her excitement, but she failed, miserably. Her expression, usually stern, was almost beaming. "I hate to give them the satisfaction of thinking they know *anything* about *anything*, but I have heard it's an amazing party every year. *And* it's our first winter formal."

Alicia nodded. "No doubt! I heard this year they are going to have a snow machine that makes real snow."

Jamie slammed her locker shut and pumped her fist. "I'm sold. I miss real snow."

Alicia sighed. "I've never seen snow, except the tacky fake kind in my front yard at Christmastime." Every year, Alicia's parents had a big Winter Wonderland party and their lawn would be covered with "snow," a kind of gross foam that took weeks to fully rinse away. Alicia had loved it when she was a kid, but now that she was older and more environmentally conscious, not so much.

Jamie's eyes grew larger. "You're kidding, right? But you guys have been to *Nueva* York."

Alicia shrugged. "With you. And it was summertime."

Jamie couldn't get the Stop the Presses expression off her face. "But it snows in Texas. And in Madrid."

Alicia shrugged once more. "Again, not when we were there."

"*Increíble,*" Jamie whispered as she held the snowflake Save the Date card up to the sky. "We've got to go to this winter formal for no other reason than for you guys to see real snow."

Alicia put her arm around her friends. "It'll be fun. And you know what the best part of this whole winter shindig is?"

She and Jamie spoke in unison. "It's a party that *we* don't have to plan!"

Jamie held up her hand for a high five, and Alicia

gave it a resounding slap. "True that," she exclaimed. Jamie and Alicia were so over the moon about going to winter formal that they neglected to notice that through their entire exchange, the usually superenthusiastic and always positive third member of their trio had remained completely silent.

While almost every morning, Alicia, Jamie, and Carmen began their day by meeting on the front steps of C. G. High, they didn't always get to end the day together as their schedules weren't always in sync. But this semester, they all had AP history as the last class of the day. It was challenging, but at least taking it together made it a bit more fun. Their teacher, Ms. Ingber, was a supermellow young woman who looked more like the teacher of a yoga class than of a tough academic one.

As Carmen and her two best friends walked into Ms. Ingber's classroom, Jamie and Alicia were still chatting about winter formal.

"I think I've forgotten how to be a guest," Jamie joked. "I'm so used to being one of the planners."

Alicia smiled. "It's easy. You pick a great dress. You put it on. You do your hair and makeup. You show up at the party and you have as much fun as humanly possible."

"Sounds pretty simple," Jamie replied as she slid into her seat. "I guess I can handle that."

Since Ms. Ingber was busy writing on the board, Jamie turned to Carmen, who was sitting right behind her, and half whispered, "Will you make my dress for the formal?"

Carmen nodded. She had perked up a bit on their way to class but was still rather subdued. Jamie and Alicia still hadn't picked up on it. "The dance is on December fifth," she said, doing the sewing calculations in her head. "That's almost two months away. No problem."

She was saved from further conversation as the bell rang and Ms. Ingber began lecturing the class on the Moorish influence in southern Spain.

Carmen was paying rapt attention to their teacher when a note came sailing across the room from Alicia, who sat two rows over from her. Alicia had folded a piece of paper into a tiny sliver so it looked like a wrapped piece of gum. Carmen unfolded it quietly and slowly so that Ms. Ingber wouldn't notice and confiscate it. When she finally got it open, she saw that Alicia had scrawled a message: *Make my dress too?*

Carmen looked over at her friend and mouthed, *Yes*.

But apparently, Carmen's skills at subterfuge did

not extend to the spylike ability to stay under the radar. Ms. Ingber had seen enough of the exchange to inquire, "Is there anything you'd like to share with the class, Miss Ramirez-Ruben?"

Carmen shook her head.

Ms. Ingber smiled. "I'll let this one slide, but let's talk after class anyway. There's something I want to discuss with you."

Carmen gulped. Was she really in trouble just for passing a note? One little teeny tiny note? She *never* got in trouble. What if Ms. Ingber said something to her mom? Maybe it was because she was a teacher herself, but Carmen's mom, Sophia, flipped over the most unlikely things. If you got a low grade on a test, it was her assumption that you had tried your best but were just struggling with the material. But if you were late for a class, or got into trouble for being disruptive, Carmen's mom would completely lose her cool. Rudeness in the classroom was a cardinal sin.

Great, Carmen thought, convinced that Ms. Ingber was going to rat her out. Just peachy. She wasn't up to having to get into it with her mother over a stupid note that she hadn't even written.

By the time the bell finally rang, Carmen was a complete wreck. She'd barely paid any attention to the lecture and jumped when Alicia darted over and poked her in the arm.

"Don't sweat it," Jamie said, joining the girls. "I'm sure it's nothing."

"Jamie's right," added Alicia. "Passing notes isn't a federal offense. Besides, you've got one of the highest averages in our class."

Carmen nodded. They were right. She'd probably worked herself up over nothing. She sighed and felt her shoulders relax—a little. The fact that they could always talk her off any ledge was one of the many things that Carmen loved about her *chicas*. "See you later," she said, as she waved good-bye to her friends.

Once the classroom had cleared, Ms. Ingber motioned to Carmen to take a seat up at the front of the classroom. "Are you familiar with the winter formal?" the teacher asked when Carmen was settled.

Carmen pulled the printed snowflake out of her notebook and nodded.

"Great, you've got your Save the Date!" her teacher said, enthusiastically. "As you know, I'm the faculty adviser for the student activities committee. *And*, as your homeroom teacher, I would love to see you get more involved with the life of the school. So, I have a great solution. With all of your experience planning *quinces*, being the assistant coordinator for the winter formal would be a breeze for you. Everyone would benefit from your talent, your leadership skills, and your business background with Amigas Inc. And if you do a good job, which I know you will, it will look great on your college applications next year."

Carmen stifled a groan. She knew she should have been relieved that Ms. Ingber wasn't chastising her about the note. And she knew that the teacher was only trying to help her out, which she appreciated. But she really didn't need more to do in her already incredibly jam-packed schedule. Plus, what her friends didn't know was that now that she and Domingo had broken up, she had no intention of even going to the dance that was sure to be the biggest romantic event of their junior year. Still, did she even have a choice? Tentatively, she asked, "What exactly does the assistant coordinator do?"

Ms. Ingber smiled and stood up from behind her desk. "Your job would be to help the Socials and Benefits Committee execute their vision. And make this the best formal C. G. High has ever seen of course."

The Socials and Benefits Committee?

The SoBees? Was she serious? Did Ms. Ingber really want her to be the lackey of the snootiest group of girls in the school?

"Thank you in advance, Carmen," she said, turning back to the papers at her desk without waiting for her to respond.

Apparently, she *didn't* have a choice. She, Carmen Ramirez-Ruben, was going to be working with the SoBees on the winter formal. There was absolutely no way for the typically optimistic Carmen to wrap this one up in a pretty bow.

It was going to be a nightmare.

CHAPTER 4

"UGH," CARMEN groaned as she slid into the restaurant booth next to Jamie later that afternoon. "So, you'll never guess what Ms. Ingber has done. She's turned me into a SoBee. She strongarmed me into working with them on the planning committee for winter formal. Might as well shoot me now."

After her meeting, Carmen had hightailed it to Lario's to join Jamie and Alicia for a much-needed rant. Lario's was their new after-school hangout. Located on Ocean Drive, it was just steps away from the sand. Since Carmen and Domingo's breakup, they had been studiously avoiding their old favorite, Bongos. It was where he and Carmen had originally met. The place was filled with too many memories for Carmen, so the girls had unanimously decided to take up residence in a new spot.

"She hates me," Carmen moaned to Jamie after

their waitress had taken their orders and walked away.

Jamie took a sip of her *agua fresca* and shook her head. "If she hated you, she wouldn't have suggested you for the committee. As irritating as the SoBees may be, she's right; it's a big deal for a junior to get that job—maybe a first—and it will look good on your college record. Which reminds me, I need to move into high gear on my extracurriculars. Plus, I have no idea who I'm going to get to write my recs next year. I may end up turning to you guys."

Carmen rolled her eyes and helped herself to a hearty serving of guacamole, salsa, and chips. "Maybe I'll get to design some scenery or paint a few signs or—hello, fun!—operate the snow machine. But I guess you're right. It can't hurt to have a teacher on my side. Maybe, if this all goes well, I can ask Ms. Ingber to write a recommendation for me to the Fashion Institute of Technology in New York," she said, trying to be positive. Her smile widened as the waitress put a plate of crispy, hot yucca fries in front of her.

Alicia, who had just walked in, nodded. "FIT would be crazy not to take you." She paused, as if uncertain whether to go on. Then she rushed ahead. "I might be out of line, but I've been thinking, maybe you should broaden your scope a little. Think about going to a liberal arts college rather than a school that specializes in fashion. So you can get a broader education, you know? The other day I read this article in *Vogue* about a girl who totally reminded me of you."

"Was she a half-Jewish, half-Catholic Latina of Argentinean descent, with five siblings?" Carmen asked, raising an eyebrow.

Alicia playfully threw a ketchup packet across the table. "No, silly. She started out studying costume design at some college in Los Angeles. She worked for a while in the wardrobe department at a movie studio and then decided that she wanted to apply her sewing skills to something completely new. She teamed up with a business partner and started a nonprofit that focuses on teaching inner-city girls how to sew and market their own clothing designs through national co-ops. But to do that, she had to go back to school, as her degree hadn't really prepared her."

Carmen looked interested, "Wow, that does sound pretty cool. *Me encanta* the idea of helping out other young women."

Jamie sipped at her virgin piña colada and adjusted the chunky silver chain necklace that she was wearing. "Alicia's right," she said, nodding. "And if you are set on New York, there are way more schools than FIT.

And way more everything that's cooler than anywhere else on the planet. You could go to NYU or Columbia or Pratt Institute; you could intern in the wardrobe department of a Broadway show, or you could work for a big fashion label."

Carmen looked back and forth between her two friends. She hadn't expected to hear this coming from them. "Those are all good ideas. And a good rec *would* go a long way toward giving me more options, I guess. So you guys think I should go ahead and work on this winter formal like Ms. Ingber asked?"

"We're professional *quince* planners," Alicia pointed out. "Planning this will be mad simple compared to most of the things we're called on to do."

Jamie polished off the goat cheese quesadilla she'd been nibbling on. "Yeah, think about it this way," she said swallowing the last bite. "With a school dance, there's no *dama* drama, no *quince* mama drama . . . no *tía* traumas . . . etc."

"No *quince*-zillas!" Alicia added.

Carmen put a hand up. "This is all true, but you are forgetting one very important thing: I will have to deal with the SoBees."

Alicia weighed both sides of the argument. "Great college rec versus snobby SoBees. It's your call."

Carmen sighed. "I guess I want the recommendation."

Just then, Jamie's phone rang, but she didn't answer it. Which was odd, because ever since Jamie had gotten the latest so-advanced-it'll-make-your-breakfast-and-run-a-bath-for-you cell, she had been almost surgically attached to it.

"Aren't you going to answer that?" Carmen asked as the phone continued to ring.

Jamie looked at the number and shrugged. "I'll call them back."

Carmen looked surprised. "Them? Don't you mean, Dash?"

"It is Dash," Jamie confirmed, looking embarrassed. "But I can talk to him later. No biggie. I'm hanging with you guys right now."

Carmen looked Jamie in the eye. "I feel like I haven't seen Dash in ages. As a matter of fact, I haven't seen Gaz in forever, either. Are you two hiding your boyfriends from me?"

Alicia blushed, which is what she did whenever she was asked a tricky question, regardless of whether or not she had something to hide. "We just want to give you time to heal," she answered softly.

Carmen loved her friends; she truly did. She

couldn't imagine two girls who were funnier, smarter, and kinder than Alicia and Jamie. But if they did not stop handling her with kid gloves because she was single again, she was going to do them some serious harm—or at the very least, stop making custom clothes for them.

Reaching into her bag for her wallet, Carmen pasted on her brightest smile. "Come on, you two, what part of '*mutual* breakup' do you not understand? I'm *fine*. And I would love to see Dash and Gaz soon, because, in addition to being your *novios*, they are also my good friends. So when are we going to hang? How about this Saturday night?"

Alicia and Jamie exchanged uncomfortable glances.

"I've got a—um—date with Gaz this weekend," Alicia offered, awkwardly. "He's taking me for a sunset cruise with dinner and dancing on a charter yacht called *The Floribbean Experience*. I know the name is cringeworthy, but I've heard it's fantastic."

Jamie looked sheepish. "Could we take a rain check? Dash has been away at an out-of-state charity golf tournament for a whole week. He gets back on Saturday, and I kind of want to be alone with him."

Carmen laughed. "No biggie, '*manitas!* Maybe we could all do brunch next Sunday."

They had finished lunch and they paid the bill. Alicia stood up and gave her friend a hug. "Sounds like a plan."

Jamie, who was never good at lingering, had already started to walk toward the front door, but she turned back. "We'll be there. Later, *amiga*."

As Carmen waved good-bye, she thought about how ridiculously her friends were behaving. She and Domingo had broken up a while ago. Sure, she still missed him. And sure, it would be nice to have a date night to look forward to—or to be able to call him and tell him about the crazy day she'd had. But she was getting used to being alone. And she had her girlfriends to talk to.

She was doing okay. Now, if only she could convince everyone else.

CHAPTER 5

A WEEK LATER, Carmen stood in front of the Setai hotel on Collins Avenue in the heart of the ocean-front district of South Beach. The SoBees, who had called a winter formal planning meeting, should have been there more than ninety minutes ago. But they were nowhere in sight.

Taking out her cell phone, Carmen dialed Dorinda's number for what must have been the tenth time that hour. When Dorinda finally picked up, she acted as if Carmen had called for your basic garden-variety chit-chat, apparently oblivious of the business that was supposed to be happening.

"Hey, Carmen, what's the *qué pasa*?" Dorinda asked. Her voice was mellow and breezy, the exact opposite of the way Carmen felt.

Carmen took a deep breath and tried to keep the agitation out of her voice. "Dorinda, I've been waiting for you guys for nearly two hours. April gave me the wrong number for her cell, and I'm pretty sure that Maya's isn't even turned on. Where are you guys?"

Carmen could hear the giggle on the other end of the line. "Don't be so high-maintenance, C.," Dorinda said. "It doesn't take four people to do one itsy-bitsy walk-through. All you need to do is check out the ball-room space where the party is going to be held. Make sure the dance floor and dining area are big enough to accommodate two hundred guests. The atmosphere has to be totally cool, and the decor needs to be so stunning that everyone at C.G. will be talking about it for the next twenty years. See? Easy peasy."

Carmen could feel herself beginning to lose the cool that had kept her from snapping in the first place. Not only were the SoBees more than ninety minutes late, they had *never* had any intention of showing up. She took a deep breath. "Dorinda. If you wanted me to do the walk-through solo, then you should have just said that in the first place."

Carmen's annoyance was apparently lost on Dorinda. "Oh, would you mind? I'd *love* for you to do the walk-through solo," she cooed. "Thanks for being such a sweetheart. *¡Hasta luego!*"

Then Dorinda hung up the phone.

Carmen looked at the END CALL message in disbelief. She began muttering to herself in Spanish: "*Ay, bendito, que perezosas.*" If Amigas Inc. had been this slack, our business would never have gotten off the ground, she thought.

This was a joke. Carmen had only been on the winter formal committee for a week, and it was clear that, while well-intentioned, Ms. Ingber had basically signed her up to be a flunky for a group of girls whose only major interest in planning the party was guessing who would be named winter formal queen. It was all just so over the top. And *so* not Carmen.

She might have agreed to be part of the committee, but that didn't mean she took the whole crowning thing seriously. It was a popularity contest, pure and simple. After only seven days, Carmen had a pretty good idea as to what had happened to the poor *chica* who had been last year's coordinator: she'd probably spontaneously combusted after the dance, in a fit of frustration and rage.

But Carmen realized she had no choice. She had signed up for this, and now she had to get to work.

Walking into the lobby of The Setai, Carmen felt as if she'd been transported to some luxurious mansion in Asia. From outside, it had looked like the typical South

Beach scene: blazing hot sun; a gazillion palm trees lining the walkways; and, as always, out of the corner of the eye, a glimpse of the beach. Inside the hotel, it was as if everything was lit by candlelight. The mixture of gray granite on the walls, chocolate velvet sofas, and Asian artifacts made you feel as if you were a million miles away from the bright, busy beach that was just outside the front door.

Despite the luxe accommodations, Carmen focused on the task at hand. If Alicia had been there, she would have flipped over the fact that the SoBees had kept the hotel events manager waiting for nearly two hours and then brazenly ditched the meeting altogether. Rule number one, which had been instituted as soon as Carmen, Alicia, Jamie, and Gaz had started Amigas Inc., was to be impeccable about your word. Don't just be on time, Alicia always said. Be fifteen minutes *early*. Don't just come in on budget. Bring the party in *under* budget. Carmen dreaded meeting the Setai hotel events manager and starting things off on such an unprofessional note. But she steeled herself for the confrontation and went to the front desk to let them know she was ready for the walk-through.

As she waited for the events manager to come down from her office, Carmen sat on the velvet sofa, near a soothing water fountain, and texted Alicia: *Please say I can quit this gig. These girls suck BIG TIME.*

Alicia wrote back immediately: Paciencia y fe. Paciencia y fe. *Will be worth it.*

Patience and faith. Carmen was going to need more than her allotted share of both to get to December without physically hurting somebody. She looked around the lobby at all the beautiful men and women who were artfully draped over sofas and tiny cocktail tables in their designer clothes and perfectly coiffed hair. Sometimes the chicest places in Miami seemed to her like a glitzed-up version of high school. Right now, the Setai hotel lobby resembled the C. G. High quad, where all the popular kids—including the SoBees—held court after school. Carmen picked up her phone again and this time texted Jamie: *The SoBees stood me up for a huge meeting at the event space. Can u believe it?*

Jamie wrote back: *Typical.*

Carmen smiled, picturing her friend in her art studio—tagging tote bags and T-shirts with her own graffiti-inspired designs. Jamie only sent back one-word texts when she was busy with her artwork. Carmen typed: *Will you teach me how to kick their butts Bronx style?*

Jamie answered: *Sure.*

Then seconds later, Jamie sent a second message: *Just chill, okay?* ☺

Carmen took a deep, cleansing breath. Chill. It was pretty good advice.

She was still practicing yoga breaths a few minutes later when the events manager, Mrs. Mantel, walked over to her.

"You must be Carmen," the woman said, extending her hand. "Pleased to meet you."

"I'm so sorry to keep you waiting, Mrs. Mantel. I know how valuable your time is."

"Please, call me Hillary," the manager insisted.

Hillary was a tall blond woman in her late twenties. She wore her hair back in a sophisticated bun, but her abstract print dress showed off an edgier side. Carmen liked her immediately. Especially after what she said next.

"Let me guess. Your classmates didn't show up," Hillary said as they walked toward the elevators.

Carmen felt her shoulders, which had been hunched up to her ears, relax. The fireworks display of anger she'd been expecting didn't seem to be coming. "How did you know?" she asked.

Hillary smiled. "I went to C. G. High before going

to undergrad and then getting an MBA degree in hospitality from Wharton. It's been my experience that members of the Socials and Benefits Committee are usually only interested in being social to the extent that it benefits *them* personally."

Carmen grinned. It was a huge relief to meet an adult who actually remembered what things were like in high school.

"So, since it is just the two of us, let me show you around," Hillary offered, as the elevator doors opened.

They traveled up to the thirty-fifth floor, where Hillary led Carmen to a door labeled THE MANDARIN ROOM.

When she walked inside, Carmen gasped. She'd seen her fair share of fancy spaces, but this ballroom was fit for a royal reception, with a plush red carpet, gold-leaf-tinged walls, and huge red and gold silk lanterns.

"This is where last year's winter formal was held," Hillary explained. "It was great. We went for a 'Paris meets Shanghai' theme: Asian food with French touches. And all the catering stations were set up like traditional Shanghai street-food carts. You've seen the pictures?"

Carmen nodded. "They were gorgeous. But they didn't do this place justice."

Hillary smiled. "It was fun. But this year, I thought you might be interested in going in an entirely different direction. Let's go up to thirty-six. There's something you should see."

As they walked up the stairs to the next floor, Hillary explained, "We've just renovated a new space. It isn't open to the public yet, but I thought you'd like to take a peek. It's not glitzy or overdone, just elegant and sophisticated, and, looking at you, I have a feeling that you might like it."

The moment the door opened, Carmen knew that the space was perfect.

It was an open plan, with chocolate brown wooden floors and metallic gray walls of poured concrete. On the far side, an expanse of industrial-looking, steel-framed windows made a rectangle around the Miami skyline. "We're calling it the New York Loft," Hillary said proudly. "And if you look out the doors, there's a wraparound deck that has nearly two thousand square feet of outside space with some of the best water views in the city."

Carmen inhaled sharply. The loft made the Mandarin Room look like an event space at a budget motel. Well, maybe not that bad, but truly, this new space was a cut above.

Carmen immediately thought of Amigas Inc. They *had* to have their next super-high-end *quince* here. But for now, it was also perfect for the winter formal—if the committee could afford it. She asked Hillary whether the loft were in the school's budget.

"Well, normally the answer would be no," Hillary said. "However, because April Yunayama is a student at your school, her dad and my boss, Mr. Yunayama, who is the owner of The Setai, has authorized me to provide C. G. High with our special Friends and Family discount rate. So, the short answer is—yes."

Carmen's eyes widened. Okay, she thought to herself, that deal alone was worth having April on the winter formal planning committee, even if her work contribution turned out to be nonexistent. But Maya and Dorinda had better start pulling their own weight.

"Perfect," Carmen said. "Our event is December fifth. How soon can I sign the contract?"

"I'll have one drafted tomorrow, and you can pick it up after school," replied Hillary.

Carmen took one last look around the New York Loft. She could already imagine the night. In that far corner, they could have a guy roasting chestnuts, just like they did in all the movies set in New York. They should definitely also have a hot chocolate station. And the snow machine could go outside the door—all the better for the one thing she was pretty sure had never happened at a C.G. winter formal: a real, honest-to-goodness snowball fight!

Hillary walked Carmen back to the lobby. Right before they parted, Carmen asked, "Just out of curiosity, where was the winter formal held when you were a student?"

The older woman smiled. "The school gym. It wasn't that long ago, but C. G. High has definitely gone from geek to chic. See you tomorrow with the contract."

With her job for the day done—well, at least one of her jobs—Carmen headed out of the hotel. She was almost out the door when she ran into two classmates: Carolina and Patricia Reinoso. Although they had the same last name, they weren't exactly sisters. They were *primas hermanas*, a Spanish term for first cousins.

Carolina had honey blond hair and flawless olive skin. She came across as a high school version of Jessica Alba, or a sun-kissed Cameron Diaz, with curves in all the right places. She was a National Merit Scholar and president of Blue and Green, C. G. High's superactive environmental group. Under Carolina's leadership, Blue and Green had done everything from proposing legislation to keep Miami's waters clean to getting a cool, green roof built for the high school. Carolina was pretty, preppy, and as far as Carmen could tell, almost perfect. And it was a sure bet in the school's halls that she'd be named winter formal queen that year, an unusual honor for a junior.

Her cousin, Patricia, was very much her gorgeous opposite. While Carolina was a blonde, Patricia was a brunette. Carolina had dark gray eyes; Patricia had dark brown eyes. While the girls had the same rocking bikini bods, Patricia was the more aggressive athlete, while Carolina's pursuits were more academic. The star center of the C. G. High girls' basketball team, Patricia was known for scoring an average of twenty to thirty points a game. She was a showboat on the court who had already attracted the attention of the WNBA. And off the court she was just as intense. She was the first girl (after Jamie) to sport a trend and the last girl to leave a party. And while Carolina was all about school spirit, dances, and crowns, Patricia didn't care one way or the other if she ever became queen of anything.

"Hey, Carmen," Carolina called out. "This is wild! I was just talking about you. You're just the girl that we needed to see."

"You needed to see *me*?" Carmen asked, looking a

bit confused. Unlike some of the other popular girls at C.G., Carolina and Patricia were nice to everyone. But even so, the girls rarely had any reason to speak to her.

"Well, we've just come from having an awesome Japanese tea service with our *mamacitas*," Carolina began, "and we've decided—"

"Well, it was my idea," Patricia said, interrupting her.

"*We* decided that we are going to have a *doble quince*," Carolina beamed, "because our birthdays are just a week apart."

"And, of course, we couldn't plan a *quince* without Amigas Inc.," Patricia pointed out. "You guys are the only ones who can give us a *quince* that will make both of us feel equally special, because even though we are supertight and our family expects us to do the same thing, you may have noticed that my *prima hermana* and I have totally different styles."

Carmen laughed. "I did sort of know that. And, well, thanks. I have to check with my business partners, but we don't have any *quinces* on our calendar right now, so this should be good timing."

She paused, confused by something. "So, wait . . . Did you guys skip a grade or something? You're both really young to be juniors."

"We went to an elementary school that had a

combined fourth and fifth grade class," explained Carolina.

"It was for so-called gifted and talented students," Patricia piped up playfully. "And because Carolina and I were so close, they let me sneak in."

"Got it. Another quick question. When are your birthdays?" asked Carmen.

"December ninth," Carolina answered.

"December seventeenth," Patricia replied.

"So, we were thinking about having the party on Saturday, December twelfth," Carolina explained.

"Right in between," Patricia added.

Carmen sighed softly. December twelfth was exactly one week after the winter formal. She could feel her stomach turning into knots. On the one hand, this was a great opportunity. What could be cooler than planning a *doble quince*? And the Reinoso girls seemed really, really chill, so she couldn't imagine too much *quince* drama. But on the other hand, between her course work, the winter formal planning, and now the rush of putting together a really big *quinceañera*, she was going to have to go without sleep until the holidays. She was exhausted just *thinking* about it.

Carmen didn't need to turn on the Weather Channel. Her own personal hurricane season had just begun.

CHAPTER 6

IT WAS DECIDED pretty quickly, given the timeline, that the cousins had to meet up with the rest of the group ASAP. An emergency meeting was called, which included the cousins' parents, and after agreeing upon a budget, they signed Amigas Inc. on as their official party-planners. For Alicia and Jamie, there was no doubt: planning the Reinoso girls' double *quince* was going to be the perfect way to end what had been an amazing year.

Although the partners in Amigas Inc. spent many weekends working on their business, being party-planners never made them feel as though they were missing out on anything. On the contrary, they often felt that they got to experience all the best parts of the fiesta, from the quiet moments when everyone arrived to the last great song the DJ played before everyone left. And the icing on the cake was that they had both a great party to plan *and* the winter formal to look forward to. Somehow, the combination of Ms. Ingber's asking Carmen to join the SoBees in planning the formal and the Reinoso sisters' contracting them to plan their *quince* made them feel a sudden rush of school pride and appreciate the pure *fun* of being juniors. They were now old enough to be confident, but at the same time, they weren't yet stressed-out seniors, obsessing about their SATs and college applications. It was the perfect time to just enjoy being in high school and not have to worry about the future.

The following afternoon, Carmen gathered the partners together for a meeting to discuss the cousins' proposal. They sat around the Cruz family pool, mulling over the possibilities. October was the tail end of the summer beach season, and the girls relished splashing around together in their swimsuits and wishing their piles of homework would magically disappear.

Alicia lay back on the sleek white pool raft and smiled. "You do know what a December *quince* means, don't you?"

Jamie nodded knowingly. "You don't have to tell me, *chica*. Extra loot for the holidays."

"I'm still not sure the payoff—no matter how big—is worth it," Carmen added. "Between winter formal, my AP classes, and this double *quince*, I'm liable to lose my mind."

"*No te preocupes*," Alicia reassured her. "Everything will be just fine. The key to keeping lots of balls in the air is to multitask. And I happen to be an excellent multitasker."

"True that," giggled Jamie. "Remember last year when I was feeling so overwhelmed just keeping up with my classes and working on Jacinda Mendez's *quince* at the same time? You were taking the lead on the party-planning, organizing a sixth grade *Harry Potter and the Goblet of Fire* school barbecue for the middle schoolers, and heading C. G. High's relief efforts for children orphaned by the earthquake in Haiti. You're so organized it gives me a headache."

Alicia laughed. "What can I say? My mom says I was born that way, that I used to organize all the activities for my toddlers' playgroup. But let's get back to it. We've got lots to do. Carm, I think you should be the contracts-and-catering point person for the Reinoso *quince*. You'll be negotiating with all the same vendors and ordering similar supplies for the formal, anyway. Plus, since you'll be bringing them twice the business, you'll probably be able to get us some sweet deals. And you know I love a *quince* that comes in under budget."

Jamie waded into the pool. "I was thinking. With two girls we have two chances of some *quince*-zilla action. Might make sense for each girl to have her own point person."

Carmen still thought the girls would probably be low-maintenance, but Alicia agreed with Jamie. She suggested that Jamie be Carolina's contact and that Carmen work with Patricia.

"And what exactly will you be doing, Señorita Cruz Control?" Carmen asked, playfully tossing a beach ball at Alicia's head.

Alicia caught the ball and threw it toward the far end of the pool, where it missed Jamie by a hair. "I will be handling the parents," Alicia said. "With two families involved, there'll be twice as many feathers to smooth. Besides, grown-ups love me."

Jamie had climbed out of the pool and, without Alicia's noticing, grabbed a cup of ice from the wrought-iron bistro table. In one swift motion she tipped the ice down Alicia's back. The other girl squealed and began jumping up and down. "Thought you were getting a little hotheaded and needed to cool off," Jamie said with a laugh.

"Not fair!" Alicia shivered. "It isn't my fault if I just *ooze* responsibility."

Not to be left out, Carmen pelted Alicia with inflatable toys from the pool. "You are such a suck-up and a Goody Two-shoes!"

It was war.

Standing up, Alicia ran for the garden hose and doused both of her friends with garden water. They shrieked and began giggling uncontrollably.

"That water is *so-o-o-o co-o-old*," Jamie laughed.

Carmen's hand-dyed cover-up was soaked through, but the smile on her face made it clear that she didn't mind at all. "This must be the oh-so-professional behavior that puts you on parent duty," she said, teasingly.

Alicia smiled wickedly, then turned the hose on her friends once more. Carmen and Jamie both rushed toward her, and as a sign of their collective maturity, they tossed her in the pool.

Carmen arrived at school early the next day hoping to have some quiet time alone in the art studio to start work on the invites for winter formal. She figured that at that hour, no one would be there to bother her and she could get enough done that she'd have time for her other work later. So, she was surprised to walk in and find Patricia and Carolina Reinoso already there, and even more surprised to find them arguing near their lockers. It was a known fact that the Reinoso cousins never argued.

Each girl held a poster featuring a flattering image of herself. One read:

LET ME BE THE QUEEN OF C. G. HIGH'S HEART
VOTE FOR PATRICIA REINOSO ON DECEMBER 5TH

And the other said:

TRUST YOUR GUT.
TRUST TRADITION.
CAROLINA REINOSO FOR WINTER FORMAL QUEEN

It would have done more harm than good to get in the middle of the argument, Carmen figured, so she slipped away and went to the art studio. For an hour, she managed to forget everything as she worked on the invites. But then the first bell rang. Sighing, she stood up, stretched, and headed out to start the day—again.

Unfortunately, while she had been sort of Zenning out, it appeared that the cousins had continued their screaming match. Dozens of students were moving past them as if in slow motion, trying to eavesdrop on the exchange.

Jamie passed the fracas and walked up to Carmen. "What's going on?" she asked, nodding in the cousins' direction.

"You got me," Carmen replied. While it was clear the two girls were fighting, it was hard to know exactly what was going on, since the growing crowd surrounding them made it difficult to hear what they were actually saying.

Jamie shook her head. "The drama can't be beginning already. We haven't even started selecting the dresses for their party. Heck, we haven't even started to come up with a theme. Should you or I be the one to tell them that they need to pace themselves? If they are already arguing now, their party will be a bust."

Carmen watched as the two girls continued to yell at each other. It was like observing someone screaming at herself in a slightly distorted mirror. Patricia and Carolina were known to be two of the prettiest girls in school. But at the moment, neither of them looked very attractive, with their fists clenched at their sides and their mouths wide open. What could have gotten them that upset? Carmen wondered.

Jamie grabbed Carmen's arm. "Let's move closer."

Carmen pulled back. "I think we're good here. They are our clients and we shouldn't get involved."

Jamie shook her head. "It's precisely because they *are* our clients that we need to tell them that they've got to stop. No one's going to come to the *quince* of the year if they think the guests of honor will be brawling on their big day."

Carmen looked incredulously at Jamie. "You think? People love drama. Look around."

There must have been more than three dozen kids gathered around Carolina and Patricia as they argued. Carmen wished she could just make everyone stop staring and go to class. But they seemed to be hanging around for the same reason she was. Having been made late for first-period class, they figured they might as well cut the class entirely.

Jamie persisted. "We've got to do something." Grabbing Carmen by the arm, she began to make her way through the crowd. It was, "Excuse me . . . pardon me . . . excuse me . . ." for a full five minutes until they were face to face with their newest clients.

Ever the brave one, Jamie walked right up to the arguing girls. "Hey, *chicas*, what's the deal?"

The two girls stopped shouting and turned, as though offended at being interrupted. But when they saw Jamie, and then the crowd that had gathered, they lowered their eyes, obviously embarrassed.

Carolina took a deep breath. "I have wanted to be winter formal queen since I was five years old. Nobody knows that more than Patricia."

"And?" Jamie said.

"*And*—now she's running, *too*," Carolina said, her dark eyes looking as though they were about to unleash a torrent of tears at any moment. "Today was the absolute last day to get on the ballot, and she sucker-punches me by announcing that she's running for queen and putting herself out there as *my* competition—"

"Do I get to say something?" Patricia interrupted. At that moment, while Carolina looked like she might cry, Patricia looked as though she were ready to get in a serious knock-down-and-drag-out fight.

"*No!* Let me finish," Carolina screeched. But suddenly, as if aware of how crazy she sounded, she softened. "We are supposed to be *primas hermanas*. A true sister wouldn't try to steal my thunder."

"Yeah? Well, a true *hermana* wouldn't be so arrogant as to think that just because she's preppy and popular means that everything should go to her," Patricia snapped.

They both turned and looked to Jamie, as if she might provide them with an answer. Jamie thought Patricia was right and that Carolina was being an entitled brat. But she knew that that wasn't the political or fair thing to say. So she suggested that they just step outside and get some fresh air.

"Carolina, why don't you go with Carmen to the snack bar on the quad?" Jamie suggested. "And Patricia, you come with me to Starbucks."

"Fine," Carolina huffed, as she walked away with Carmen.

"An excellent idea," Patricia said as she and Jamie headed for the south exit of the school.

It was Carmen's third year at Coral Gables High School, but, as hard to believe as it was, she'd never eaten at the snack bar on the quad. It was sort of known as the cool kids area, and she'd never needed a snack badly enough that she'd have risked feeling uncomfortable. Now, as she walked toward it with Carolina, she felt just a little bit nervous. As usual, the tables were dominated by the jocks, cheerleaders, and other popular kids who occupied their stratosphere.

Everyone nodded to Carmen, but it was Carolina they called out to. "Hey, Carolina, looking good, *Mami*," Alfonso Carew, the school's star baseball player, bellowed. Carolina smiled and waved.

Once at the snack bar, Carolina ordered a latte, and

Carmen followed suit. Then they took their drinks and sat at a table away from the various crowds.

"We could use a little privacy, don't you think?" Carolina suggested. Carmen nodded her head in agreement.

But that was, it seemed, too much to ask. No sooner had they sat down than they were descended upon by the SoBees. April, Dorinda, and Maya had clearly begun their day with a morning wardrobe text, because the three were dressed nearly identically in expensive-looking floral-print jumpsuits and towering gladiator heels.

"Are we late?" Dorinda asked rhetorically as she slid into a seat next to Carolina. "I'm assuming that this is the war room for your winter formal–queen campaign."

"It's not a war room," Carolina said, politely but firmly.

"Of course it's not," April replied. "But that's what we love about you. You're not at all overly aggressive and competitive. You're humble, which is a lovely quality to have in a queen."

Carolina took a sip of her coffee, but not before Carmen noticed a look of sharp impatience flash across her face. So Carolina wasn't as infatuated with the SoBees as their own gossip would have led one to believe. This was interesting information, Carmen thought, anxious to share the news with Jamie and Alicia. She would also have to report that hanging out with the SoBees was like watching a sociology video. They had their own language, their own sort of code, and they definitely had their favorite activities—the most popular of which was playing nice with people— even if they didn't really like said people.

"Love your shoes!" April exclaimed, peering down at Carolina's patent-leather platform pumps. "Who are they?"

"Jimmy Choo," Carolina mumbled.

Maya, April, and Dorinda swooned in unison. "It's like we always say," April said, twirling the long gold chain around her neck. *"It's not a shoe, unless it's Jimmy Choo."*

Carolina smiled tightly. "Listen, you guys, I really need to talk to Carmen about some stuff for my *quince*, and I've got Latin American lit in fifteen minutes, so would you mind excusing us?"

If the SoBees felt dismissed, they didn't show it.

"Of course!" Dorinda said, bussing each of Carolina's cheeks. "We'll leave you to it. Your *quince* is going to rock. Make sure to send out those Save the

Dates, though. It's Fabulous season in Miami, and you know how we girls like to stay busy."

April and Maya gave Carolina air-kisses and then inexplicably blew a kiss at Carmen. As they turned to walk away, Maya gave Carmen's shoulder a squeeze. "This little one is a gem. I don't know how we'd survive without her."

Little one? Carmen was five feet nine inches tall! And why were they suddenly being so nice to her? Had she entered some sort of snack-bar-related alternate reality?

Pushing aside her confusion at the sudden change from snarky to sweet, Carmen turned back to Carolina. "Okay, so tell me," Carmen said. "What's up with you and Patricia? Are we going to have to put a stop to this *quince* before we have even begun?"

Carolina shrugged. "Patricia's competitive. That's who she is. She always has to put herself out there. That's why she loves basketball so much. It's not her against one other person—which is like my sport, singles tennis—she'd much rather take on a whole team."

Carolina shook out her impressive mane of hair. Then she went on, "Look, I'm not completely ignorant. I know that for a lot of people, the queen and king thing is sort of retro and irrelevant. I'm smart. I want to get my PhD in public health policy someday. I've got a brain and a heart and a soul. But I'm also a girl who loves dressing up. I'm a girl who loves romance and princess movies, and I've *always* wanted to be crowned queen of winter formal. And if I were chosen this year, it would be the best *quince* gift I could ever wish for.

"Patricia is a star on the court," Carolina continued. "*I* want to be the belle of the ball. Just once. Patricia knows how much it means to me. I never in a million years would have thought she'd do this—sign up and everything—just because she can."

Listening to the other girl speak, Carmen was reminded of Alicia and Jamie. They were both so close, but, like Carolina and Patricia, so, *so* different. For a long time, Jamie had thought Alicia was rubbing her nose in it that her family was well off and Jamie's was not. And for an equally long period of time, Alicia had thought Jamie had a chip on her shoulder about money. Carmen had played referee between the two of them long enough to know that in any riff between close friends, chances were good that nobody meant to be vicious and that both parties were equally hurt.

Carmen took a sip of her latte, which had gotten just cold enough not to taste good, but not cold enough to pass for iced coffee. "Is it possible," she asked hesitantly, "that because you guys are *primas hermanas*, because you are more than friends—you're family—that maybe there is more going on than just Patricia trying to hurt you for some reason, and maybe you just haven't seen it *because* you're so close? That maybe she has a reason of her own for really wanting this crown, too?"

Carolina's eyes flashed, and Carmen knew her words had touched a nerve.

"You don't get it," Carolina said, her dark gray eyes filling with tears. "Everything I have—the good grades, the friends, the clothes—I've had to work really, really hard for. Patricia is one of those lucky people who never plan or struggle for anything, but everything turns out perfectly for them all the same. For once, there was something I thought I could do and have just turn out perfectly. And now that chance is gone."

Carmen handed the girl a tissue and gave her a hug. "I'm going to be completely honest with you," she said. "I think Patricia has a right to run for winter formal queen. It's a free country; she can do what she wants. But I also think that you are tougher than you think. You're not just any pretty, popular girl. You're a rock star, inside and out. *You* are the winter formal queen our school deserves."

Carolina's eyes widened as she used the tissue Carmen handed her to wipe her tears away. "Do you really think so?"

Carmen nodded. "I know so. Consider me your first fan. I'm on Team Carolina. And together, we are going to make you a belle!"

CHAPTER 7

OVER AT STARBUCKS, Patricia was busy giving Jamie her side of the story. Which sounded eerily similar to Carolina's tale of woe. The crux of Patricia's complaint was that her cousin had been the family favorite since the day she was born.

"She was born a week ahead of me, and I feel like I've been playing catch-up ever since," Patricia complained. "Carolina is that picture-perfect, cashmere-sweater-wearing, tennis-playing, honor-roll girl. She can do no wrong. I, on the other hand, am constantly trying to prove myself."

Jamie could identify with Patricia's outsider perspective. Even though she'd moved to Miami at the end of junior high and had known Alicia and Carmen almost as long as she'd known anybody, Jamie still felt a bit like an outsider around them, as though she could never make up for the history that they had built together, or the ease with which they navigated Miami's social circles. Yes, her boyfriend was a rising golf star. Yes, she spent more time at country clubs and resorts than she had ever in her life imagined she would, thanks to Dash, and yes, because of him, wherever they went together, people treated them like royalty. But part of Jamie always resented girls like Carolina, whose money and looks got them everywhere they wanted to go.

Of course, the truth was that Patricia was no less privileged than her cousin. But in her own story, she'd cast herself as the underdog, which meant that she had a fan in Jamie.

"Is it true that you've known since you were kids that Carolina had this big dream of being winter formal queen one day?" Jamie asked before slurping down the remainder of her iced chai tea, which, to her chagrin, was mostly ice.

Patricia shrugged. "So, she wanted to be winter formal queen. Big whoop! Is nobody else supposed to run? If she's the queen that the school wants this year, then she should have no problem with a little friendly competition."

Jamie couldn't have agreed more. "I'll help you out. I believe in shaking things up."

And just like that, Jamie Sosa, née Jamie of the

boogie-down Bronx, became not only the *quince* planner for both Reinoso girls, but a behind-the-scenes campaign manager for Patricia's winter formal queen campaign.

It wasn't until Patricia had left, taking off running toward her Spanish class, that Jamie realized that she had never gotten to ask Patricia why she wanted to be winter formal queen. Why the sudden change of heart? But that was okay, she figured. There'd be plenty of time to ask later.

None of the members of Amigas Inc. had time to catch up for the rest of that day. Carmen was busy with SoBee-related work, Alicia had promised she'd attend an art exhibit with her mother after school, and Jamie was way behind on some work for her Etsy site. So it wasn't until the next morning, on the way to class, that Jamie even saw Carmen. But when she did, her eyes narrowed. Her friend was holding some suspicious-looking boards with bright lettering all over them.

"What are those?" Jamie asked.

Carmen shrugged. "Just some winter formal stuff for Carolina. She asked me to help her out." It was now her turn to grow suspicious. Because Jamie was holding on to something as well. Pointing at the banners draped over Jamie's arm, Carmen asked, "And those?"

"I'm helping Patricia with her campaign," Jamie replied matter-of-factly.

If anyone had been standing close to the two friends at that moment, he or she would have felt a distinct chill in the air. The girls looked at each other, eyes still narrowed. Carmen had her free hand on her hip, while Jamie had cocked her head, as if to say, *Wanna make something of it?*

"Um, correct me if I'm wrong," Carmen said, "but you're Super Art Girl, and Patricia's a client. You should be helping both girls."

Jamie instantly reacted. "Pot calling the kettle black much? What about you, then? Why are you helping Carolina? Besides, Patricia's not just a client. She's my new friend—*and* the next winter formal queen."

To which Carmen replied, "Well, we'll see about that."

Lunchtime found Alicia and Gaz in the cafeteria. They were sharing an enormous Cuban sandwich chock-full of ham, roasted pork, Swiss cheese, pickles, mustard, and salami.

Gaz had just taken a huge bite of his lunch, some of which ended up on his cheek. Alicia affectionately wiped a smidgen of mustard off his face, and was about to give him a quick kiss when a shadow descended over the table—in the form of Carmen and Jamie. The two girls were scowling, arms folded across their chests.

"What's the *qué pasa, chicas*?" Gaz asked, sensing as much as Alicia did that something was wrong.

That was all it took. The girls immediately went at it, talking over one another as they each tried to tell their side of the story. From what Alicia and Gaz could make out, each was arguing that the other had crossed the line by offering her support to the opposing winter formal queen candidate.

After three minutes of loud yelling, Alicia had had enough. "I feel like I'm on *Law and Order*," she said, banging an imaginary gavel. "Order in the court! Order in the court! Step up to the bench and state your case."

"Come on, Lici," Jamie pleaded. "This is serious. Girls like Carolina think they're entitled to be queen of this and queen of that just because they have blond hair and blue eyes and fit the preppy, popular-girl mold."

Carmen shook her head, incredulous. "As if! Carolina isn't a cookie-cutter popular girl. She's no SoBee. She isn't a cheerleader. She's president of an environmental group. Being queen of the winter formal is something she's wanted from the time she was a little girl. Patricia is just being a hater by entering at such a late date."

Alicia held up her hands. "As entertaining as it is to watch you two go at it like four-year-olds, this is bad for business. You need to let Patricia and Carolina handle their own campaigns. Our job is to keep them focused on one thing and one thing only: the most important day of their lives—their *quinceañera*. Case closed."

Carmen and Jamie exchanged hard looks. Alicia's advice was sound, but neither of them had any intention of backing down. They were only just beginning.

After lunch, Carmen raced across the quad to her next class. She had so much to do that her head was spinning. There was a winter formal meeting at 3:15. Then, at 5:30, a meeting with the Reinoso cousins was on tap, and after that it was home to tackle a paper comparing identity and depiction of self in the poetry of Walt Whitman and Willie Perdomo. Just thinking about it all made her tired.

Somehow, she had managed to make it to her next class. But try as she might to pay attention, the exhaustion was just too much, and she let out a huge yawn. Unfortunately, it was at that very moment that her advanced biology teacher, Mr. Julian, walked by her desk.

"Am I boring you, Ms. Ramirez-Ruben?" he asked. "I do try so very hard to be interesting."

Carmen sighed. If she had had a dime for every time a teacher used that *Am I boring you?* line, she'd have been as rich as a celebutante. Didn't teachers remember what high school was like? How the mad rush of classes and papers and activities and a part-time job could run a girl ragged?

Obviously not. Carmen shook her head and smiled sweetly. "I apologize, Mr. Julian." Luckily he seemed to be in a forgiving mood and simply nodded. He walked away, continuing his scintillating lecture on one-celled organisms.

When what seemed like eons later, the bell finally rang, Carmen snapped her book shut and took off again across the quad as fast as her legs would carry her.

The SoBees were sitting at the snack bar all dressed up in matching Palm Beach–style sundresses. Judging by the way they languorously sipped their lattes, it was as if they'd been sitting in the quad all afternoon without a care in the world.

"How'd you get here so fast?" Carmen asked, out of

breath and feeling closer to gym-class sweaty than she would have liked.

The SoBees smiled pityingly. While Carmen was nearly six feet tall, the SoBees had a way of making her feel as if she were back in the third grade and the smallest kid in the class.

"We never sign up for a class during last period," Maya explained, as she multitasked, reapplying a fuschia lip gloss while flipping through the pages of *People* magazine.

"But you've got to take something," Carmen asked, confused.

"Duh. We have study hall," Dorinda explained. "Two p.m. study hall is monitored by Mrs. Clarke, and she never takes attendance."

April piped up. "That way, if we've got to bounce early—to go shopping or to spin class or to meet up with some hotties from another school, then we can be out, no prob."

"Wow," Carmen said, taking this information in. Some kids seemed born gaming the system, and clearly, the SoBees could count that among their many charming skills. "I'll be right back."

Carmen walked over to the quad snack bar and bought herself a soda. Not the healthiest thing in the world, but she needed the caffeine.

She rejoined the SoBees and took a checklist out of her oversize hobo bag. "We have a ton of work to do—"

"My thought exactly," Dorinda said, taking the checklist away from Carmen and using it as a coaster for her latte. "First things first, though. Who are we going to support for queen?"

April looked up from her brand-new hot pink iPad and gave her friend a "duh" look. "Is there any question? Carolina. She's pretty. She's smart. She's stylish. And she's our friend."

Maya nodded. "I couldn't agree more. I met Shakira once at the radio station, and she looks a little bit like her. Carolina is right out of the C.G. handbook. She's the definition of 'queen.'"

Carmen, unaware that there was such a thing as a C.G. handbook, made a mental note to check it out. She moved Dorinda's coffee and retrieved her checklist. "You guys, can we focus? There are about a hundred things to do on this list, and we're only weeks away from the big event. I know I'm new at this, but it seems like we've got a lot more important things to discuss than who's going to be queen."

Dorinda, Maya, and April exchanged glances, then

burst out laughing. Then Dorinda reached over and patted Carmen's arm, as though soothing a crying baby. "Silly, the whole point of the winter formal is to elect the queen. We have to make sure the queen is as wonderful as the dance."

Carmen could barely suppress a groan. These girls were nuts. "I *thought* the whole point of the winter formal was to create a magical evening that our classmates will never forget."

Dorinda placed her fingers, in the shape of a *W*, on her forehead. "Whatever. They'll never forget the winter formal, because it's when we crown the queen."

Carmen took a deep breath. This was going nowhere. And even though Carmen was now as invested as the SoBees were in her candidate's becoming winter formal queen, she knew from all her experience planning *quinces* how much work and coordination it took to plan for such a big event. The crowning was only one small piece of the puzzle.

But if all the SoBees cared about was the contest and the girl who wore the crown, then, fine. She would whip them into shape by speaking their language and would couch all of her requests in terms of the way it affected the crowning of the queen.

"*O-o-o-o*-kay, Dorinda," Carmen crooned, in the

calmest voice she could summon. "And do you care at all about what kind of decorations are on the wall or what kind of food is served when the queen is crowned?"

Dorinda shrugged. "Hmmm. Let me think about that. . . . Not really."

Okay, so maybe there was no common language. Carmen was at her wit's end. "Well, who do you think is going to pull all of this together?" she asked, jumping to her feet and waving the checklist in the air.

"You," Dorinda replied, almost sweetly. "That's why Ms. Ingber assigned you to be the project manager. She knew that you were the perfect person to get the job done. We always find a super-duper *workabee* to pull all the party details together for us."

Dorinda stood up and threw her coffee cup into the trash. "Meeting's over."

April looked at her watch and grimaced. "OMG! We're late. It's the Last Call sale at Neiman Marcus, and there is a pair of sixty percent–off stilettos with my name on it." She turned to Carmen briefly to add, "But good job on being so organized."

Maya stood up as well, and she and April tossed their coffee cups into the trash with basketball player–like precision.

"I love you for being such a kick-ass project manager," Maya said insincerely before giving Carmen a never-touch-the-skin air-kiss.

"That checklist is *genius*," Dorinda added.

And with that, the SoBees walked off. For a few minutes Carmen just sat in the quad, stunned. How did they do it? How did they saddle her with all of the work and make it seem like they'd all just had a lovely afternoon tea? Before she'd spent any time with them, Carmen had assumed that the SoBees were like any members of a superpopular clique: self-obsessed, shallow, ever so slightly mean-spirited, and not very bright. But now that she'd gotten to know them a little bit, Carmen looked at the SoBees with newfound respect. They weren't stupid. And they weren't merely shallow. They were like the girls from the classic movie *Heathers*. Evil geniuses. More specifically, they were *lazy* evil geniuses who had somehow gotten her to do their bidding.

How many of her older brother's comic books had she read over the years? Dozens, possibly hundreds. Really, having done all that reading, she should have seen the evil geniuses coming.

CHAPTER 8

AT 5:10 THAT evening, Carmen sprinted from school to the bus stop and then waited nearly an hour for the bus to South Beach. She felt like the White Rabbit in *Alice in Wonderland*. She was late, very late, for a very important date. Even though she was wearing heels, the minute the bus pulled up to her stop, she got out and sprinted toward Las Ramblas. She loved living in Miami, but without a ride from Gaz, her brother, her older siblings, or her parents—all the lucky people she knew who were old enough to drive *and* own a car— getting around town was sort of miserable. That was one thing she'd forgotten over the last year, while she was dating Domingo. He'd been a senior in high school (she was a sophomore), with a license and a set of wheels, a classic red and white Mini Cooper that he'd gotten for a steal because his brother-in-law ran a used-BMW dealership. She'd felt so cool in Domingo's car. Running down Ocean Drive now at the speed of light? Not so much.

Her mood didn't improve when she arrived at the restaurant. From the look of things and the icy stares the cousins were shooting at each other, it was clear that the Reinoso girls were still on the outs. Carolina sat next to Alicia and sulked. Patricia sat on the other side of Jamie, cross-armed and furious-looking. Who knew that party-planning could feel so much like combat duty, Carmen thought as she speed-walked over to the table. She slid into the booth next to Carolina. She knew that she shouldn't choose favorites, but she had to admit that bookish Carolina was more her kind of girl than Patricia, the popular jock.

"Sorry I'm late," Carmen apologized. She glanced at Alicia and was relieved to see that her friend did not look stressed by her tardiness.

"Don't sweat it," Alicia said. "The buses were terrible today."

The girls shared a moment of commiseration about Miami's atrocious public transportation.

"*Quinceañeras* are hot," Jamie said, "don't get me wrong. But I can't wait until sweet-sixteen time, when I can get a real driver's license."

Carmen sighed. "I've been so busy that I haven't

even gotten my learner's permit."

"Which one of your parents is going to teach you how to drive?" Carolina asked, speaking up for the first time since they'd sat down.

"Well," Carmen began—because the question really wasn't as easy as it would have appeared—"I have four parents. My dad is a *telenovela* producer who gets driven to and from the set half the time by some hapless production assistant. So he's out. The only reason he would teach me would be to turn me into his chauffeur. My stepmother, Natalia, is an actress and kind of a big star in Venezuela. She already thinks that my brother and sister and I are the hired help. She'd probably just teach us how to tip the valet at her favorite spas and salons. My stepfather, Christian, is British, and while he's lived in Miami for practically forever, I'm pretty sure that just the way you can see my Grandmother Ruben translating from Spanish to English when she talks, Christian is mentally switching the road back and forth while he drives. . . ."

"So that leaves your mom, right?" Alicia said. She turned to the cousins. "You guys know Carmen's mom?"

"Head of the math department, right?" Patricia replied, nodding. "I had her for integrated algebra, and I worked my butt off for a C-plus."

Patricia was right. Carmen's mom could be a taskmaster—in the classroom and at home. Which was why Carmen was just a little nervous about having her help teach her to drive. When Carmen's older sister, Una, was learning how to drive, their mom actually made her take a tape measure and measure the distance from the car to the curb, the bumper to the fire hydrant, and one car to another when they were seated in traffic. Una and their mom barely spoke to each other for weeks after Una failed her driver's test the second time. Carmen took a deep breath. All this talking and thinking about the learning process made public transportation look pretty darned good.

With the small talk over, the girls moved on to the next order of business: the menu. They ordered half a dozen small plates of various items to share at the table: fried calamari, garbanzo beans with chorizo, sautéed clams, seafood paella, and Spanish potato-and-spinach tortillas.

While they all sat starving and somewhat distracted by the enticing smells coming from the kitchen, Alicia used the lull in activity as an opportunity to get to the real reason they were there: the *quinceañeras*.

Amigas Inc. had planned so many *quinceañeras* that they had more than enough expertise to walk the birthday girls through the experience. The most important decision, the one that would affect everything, from the *quince* dress to the food and decorations, was picking a theme. That was what needed to happen today. Alicia passed out the folders with theme topics that Jamie and Carmen had compiled with their own original Amigas Inc. logo on the cover.

"This is exciting," Carolina said, flipping through the checklist and the photos of former clients enjoying their special day.

"It's pretty haute," Patricia said. "Haute," as in haute couture, was fashion-conscious South Beach slang for *hot*.

"So, let's talk about your theme," Alicia said. "What do you have in mind?"

Carolina and Patricia said, simultaneously, "I want a princess theme."

Carolina added, "After all, I'll be looking for places to wear my crown."

And just like that, it was back to rough waters.

Patricia turned to Jamie. "Do you see what I mean?" she hissed. "Señorita Spoiled Rotten just assumes she's going to win."

You could practically see the steam coming out of Carolina's ears. "No, what I assume is that if there's something I really want, you're going to want it, too."

Carmen had had enough stress for one day. Trying to defuse the tension, she said, "Look, *chicas*, we don't really do princess-themed *quinces*. So there is no reason to fight over that idea anyway. Not if you are going to stick with us."

Jamie passed around the platter of salsa *verde* and chips. "Yeah, we kind of have a no-princess rule. It's not creative enough."

Carolina and Patricia exchanged glances, and for a moment they seemed to put their feuding aside. "But it's our *quince*, right?" Patricia said, tentatively.

"Isn't the customer always right?" Carolina added.

"*Absolutamente*," Alicia agreed. "But if you really want something as basic as a princess theme, then you don't need the Amigas, you just need an hour-long pit stop at any ol' party shop."

Carolina and Patricia thought for a moment, and then, with the quiet understanding that two girls who have been raised practically as sisters develop, they said in unison, "Nope, we give in."

Patricia looked at her cousin tenderly, the earlier anger evaporating, and said, "We want it to be special."

"We've been dreaming about this since we were little," Carolina added. "We want it to be unique."

"Okay, great, then that's settled. No princesses. How many guests are you planning on having?" Jamie asked Patricia.

"I don't know," Patricia mused. "What's average? A hundred guests?"

Everyone said that they wanted a small *quince*, but truthfully, a *quince* was one of those rare occasions when economies of scale dictated that it made as much sense to have a ton of people as it did to have just a few. As it was, if you had the traditional court, it was seven girls, seven guys, and the honoree made the fifteenth person. Even if you just added those in the immediate family, then you were looking at another five people. That was twenty people right there. And that was before you'd even included your dear old *abuela*, or your cousins on both sides, or your dad's best friend from childhood, whom you called Tío because he was like the cool uncle you never had.

If you invited classmates, then social graces—and good manners—dictated that you invite the whole class. Whether it was everyone in your econ class or all the girls on your soccer team, that was another twenty kids, more if they brought dates. Which meant that at the end of the day, any girl whose family had made the financial commitment to a big blowout *quinceañera* was looking at inviting a staggering number of people. Patricia wasn't far off—a hundred guests was just about right . . . as a starting point!

But there was one difference in this case. Alicia pointed to Patricia and said, "A hundred guests for you." Then she turned to Carolina and said, "Plus, a hundred guests for you. That's two hundred guests in total—minimum. Two hundred and twenty-five, if we leave ourselves some wiggle room for uninvited tag-alongs and well-meaning party crashers."

"There's bound to be some numbers-swelling in a party this size," Jamie noted as she took a sip of her Arnold Palmer, a lemonade-and-iced-tea drink (named after the legendary golf player) to which she'd become addicted since dating Dash.

"Exactly. Which means we need a venue—a big one," Alicia said, flipping through the photo file of event spaces she kept on her iPod.

"If we weren't holding the winter formal there, the New York Loft at The Setai would be perfect," Carmen said.

Patricia looked interested. "I like the idea of a loft space. I want something a little dark, cutting-edge, cool."

"I was thinking, if we aren't going with a princess

theme, a beach *quince* might be nice," Carolina said tentatively. "Outdoors. Something tropical and sweet. Tiki lights. Lots and lots of flowers."

The easy feeling that had settled over the table went away again as Patricia scowled. "A beach *quince*?" she scoffed. "Picture me trying to walk across the sand in stiletto heels. No way.

"It's too bad winter formal isn't sooner," she growled, ripping a paper napkin to shreds. "That way, the queen could decide what kind of *quince* she wanted to have."

Carolina snorted. "If the queen gets to choose, then not only would we have a beach *quince*, but I'd advise you to get a waterproof dress, because me and my *damas* might have to make sure you go for a little swim. You do like exercise, right, *prima*?"

Patricia stood up, looking as if she were ready to exercise more than just her freedom of speech.

Jamie, who knew a thing or two about losing your cool at inopportune moments, put a reassuring hand on Patricia's shoulder. "Chill, *chica*," Jamie said. "*No vale la pena*. It's not worth it."

While the *primas hermanas* bickered, Carmen was quietly going through winter formal files on her iPad, on loan from the school's events office. Smiling, she looked up. "I've got it," she said. "The solution to all of our problems."

Patricia, still hot under the collar, asked, "Does it involve feeding all the snobs at the table to a Miami gator?"

Carolina's eyes narrowed. "You are so childish," she hissed.

"Says the girl who threatened to dunk me at my own *quince*," Patricia shot back.

"Order in the court, order in the court," Carmen called out, using the unopened bottle of Pellegrino on the table as a gavel.

Carmen held up her iPad: "Exhibit A, the Biltmore, one of Coral Gables's oldest, most beautiful hotels."

Alicia nodded. "I'd forgotten all about the Biltmore. We've always wanted to have a *quince* there."

"Well, now's our chance. It's gorgeous," Jamie said, approvingly. "What do you think, Patricia?"

"It's kind of like something out of *Twilight*," she said, looking at the photos. "Like an old castle. I like it."

Carolina was determined to disagree with her cousin. "It's not like *Twilight* at all. It's more like a royal fairy-tale setting."

Carmen sighed. "Does that mean you like it?"

Carolina nodded. "It's the perfect setting to celebrate

my victory as winter formal queen."

Before Patricia could respond, Carmen jumped up and said, "Okay, now we need a theme, and I propose . . . Exhibit B."

She held up the iPad again. "A masked ball, like the kind they have every year in Venice. The dress code is eighteenth-century formal: powdered wigs, corsets, hoop gowns, the works."

There was silence.

"What do you think?" Carmen was a little nervous that the *primas* would be so intent on squabbling that their planning for the *quinceañera* would be totally sidetracked.

"I like it," Patricia finally said. "The mask should cover up all of her ugly."

Apparently, that was just too much for Carolina to handle. All the anger vanished, and she looked as if she had been slapped. Her eyes filled with tears.

Carmen, the middle child in an extended family of six, had been playing the role of referee her entire life. "That's enough. Clearly, you two have some issues to work through. Until you can do that, this meeting— and any potential party-planning—is over. We can handle *quince* drama. But we don't tolerate mean girls or divas."

Patricia stared down at her lap. "I'm sorry, Carolina," she muttered softly. "I didn't mean it."

Carmen shot Patricia a look that said, *Not good enough!*

"Okay, *lo siento*," Patricia said. "I really am sorry. I'm not trying to be a jerk. Maybe this whole thing is stressing me out more than I thought."

"It's okay," Carolina mumbled, still looking vulnerable, but starting to recover as color came back slowly to her cheeks.

Sitting at the table, Alicia and Jamie exchanged glances. They were not used to seeing this take-charge side of Carmen. Maybe Ms. Ingber had been right to sic the SoBees on their friend. Or maybe, just maybe, it was the other way around. And Ms. Ingber had actually known that Carmen—quiet, confident, capable—was the perfect girl to whip the SoBees into shape.

CHAPTER 9

EMBOLDENED by the authority she'd shown in the Patricia–Carolina squabble, Carmen walked into the next day's winter formal meeting full of confidence—and plans. The SoBees were waiting for her in the library, idly buffing their nails and checking their e-mail on their phones.

"Hey," Maya said, not looking up from her fanzine.

"*Hola*," Dorinda waved as she scrolled through her Facebook wall.

"Yoo-hoo," April trilled as she touched up her manicure.

"Look," Carmen said, as she slammed her books down on the table. "I know you guys are fabulous and that you usually have someone else doing your bidding. But my being assistant coordinator does *not* mean that I'm going to do all the work for you. The winter formal is a huge event, and everyone has to pitch in."

Carmen reached into her bag for a sheaf of papers and passed them out. "Here are your assignments. Maya, you have all the music connects. You're in charge of booking the band. My friend Gaz can help you figure out who's local, who's good, and who's affordable. In that order."

Maya made a face. "But I am so *swamped*."

Carmen raised her hand as if she were a traffic cop directing a car to stop. "I have three words to say to you: Cute. Boy. Musicians. Now, stop complaining."

Maya smiled and pretended to salute Carmen. "Yes, sir. I mean, yes, ma'am."

Carmen walked over to April. "You are now in charge of food."

April began to fiddle with the pearls around her neck. "But I'm not *into* food. And my dad did hook us up with the room at the hotel. And—"

Carmen interrupted. "Before you start to make a lot of noise, I have three words to say to you: Cute. Boy. Chefs."

"Well, when you put it that way . . ." April acquiesced.

Dorinda, the queen bee of the SoBees, looked imperious and unimpressed in her sky-high stilettos, white jeans, and jacket—which Carmen could tell was a real one.

"Who died and left you the boss of everything?" Dorinda asked.

"Well, when you decided to do absolutely nothing to plan this party, you did," Carmen retorted.

Dorinda stuck her hand out and waited for Carmen to hand her a folder similar to the ones that April and Maya had received. "Fine," Dorinda conceded. "What's my assignment?"

Carmen smiled. If she'd only known that being bossy could yield such incredible results, she really would have tried it sooner. "Since you're so into it, your job is to secure all the flair for the queen and her court—everything from crowns to sashes."

Reaching into her bag, Carmen took out a simple silver tiara and placed it on Dorinda's perfectly coiffed head.

"What's this?" Dorinda asked.

"A sample from one of the vendors that Amigas Inc. has worked with in the past."

April gave her friend an appraising look. "I like it," she said.

Carmen grinned. "I thought you would."

As the SoBees walked out with their marching orders, Carmen let out a breath she hadn't realized she'd been holding. Then she cracked open her Latin

American literature book and looked at her watch. She could squeeze in half an hour of studying before her next meeting. But just as she was getting into it, she was approached by Ms. Ingber.

"That was some impressive delegating," the teacher said, patting Carmen on the shoulders. "I told you C. G. High needed those leadership skills."

And, for the first time since she'd begun this whole crazy thing, Carmen had to agree.

The next day was Saturday, and after a busy week of studying, wrangling SoBees, and *quinceañera* planning, Carmen was ready for a break. For the first time in the two months since she and Domingo had parted, she was feeling like her old self and ready to have some serious fun. She texted Jamie and Alicia: *Where my girls at? Let's hang tonight.*

Two hours later, when she hadn't heard back, she texted again: *Code blue, code blue, where is my crew?*

This time, the response was immediate. Alicia wrote: *Sorry,* chica. *My parents are hosting some Latino political alliance dinner. Got to stay home and fight the good fight.*

Minutes later, Jamie texted: *Sorry to be incog-*latino. *In the studio. Feeling too creative to hang.*

Carmen sighed and threw her long legs over the stool in her family's kitchen. That was the problem with having friends who were so fabulous. They always had something going on.

Her mother walked into the room and asked, "Why the long face, *hija*?"

Carmen shrugged. "Alicia and Jamie are busy, and I kind of want to go out."

Sophia smiled. "Me, too. Let's go see a movie. Something incredibly romantic and cheesy that Christian wouldn't see with me."

Carmen brightened. It had been ages since she and her mom had gone out, just the two of them. "Awesome. Sounds like a plan."

Just then, Christian entered the room, in time to catch the tail end of the conversation. He was tall, blond, and handsome. Like a British George Clooney.

"What's the plan?" he asked.

"We're going to see *I Love You, Too, Puppy* at the multiplex," Sophia replied.

Christian made a face. "Is that the movie about two dogs and their ridiculous owners who hate each other but then fall in love?"

"*Exactamente.* We'd love for you to join us," Carmen's mother smiled sweetly.

Her husband shook his head. "That's quite okay. Manchester United is playing on the telly down at the Kingsley Arms. I'll be there."

The Kingsley Arms was a British pub in Coral Gables that not only showed European soccer games featuring teams like Manchester United, Christian's favorite childhood team, but also served all kinds of British food that Carmen just did not get—like bangers and mash and Heinz spaghetti on toast.

"I love your arroz con pollo," Christian said, giving Carmen's mother a hug, "but sometimes a man needs a good old-fashioned shepherd's pie."

"Have fun," her mother said, waving him off.

"Go, go, Reds!" Carmen called out, referencing the red jersey that the Manchester players wore.

Tickets for the eight p.m. show in hand, Carmen and her mother were standing in the concession-stand line, trying to decide what kind of sugary treat they'd have, when Carmen heard a familiar voice behind her.

A familiar, *male* voice.

She turned around to see Domingo standing hand in hand with a girl she didn't recognize. The girl was pretty. Older. Eighteen, maybe nineteen. Everything about her said college, not high school, from her expertly flat-ironed hair to her crisply ironed button-down shirt and expertly tailored jeans. No one in high school ironed their shirt for a movie on a Saturday night, not even Carmen, and fashion was her business. Looking at the girl, so pretty, so grown-up, *so* holding Domingo's hand as if it belonged to her, Carmen's heart sank. She felt as if she'd been shoved into a pool and that she was falling deeper and deeper, shocked and gasping for air.

Domingo had been saying something to the girl but, as if sensing Carmen's presence, he looked up and locked eyes with her. His expression was unreadable.

"What's up, Carmen?" he said softly. "*Buenas noches,* Señora R."

Carmen nodded, but her heart was still drowning. She'd been fine about the breakup. It had been mutual. At least, that was what she kept telling Alicia and Jamie. If it were true, why was she so devastated seeing Domingo and some random girl?

"What are you doing here?" she finally sputtered, the words sounding way shakier than she meant them to.

"We get a long weekend for Columbus Day," the girl said, answering for Domingo. She had a southern accent, and her words spilled out of her mouth like syrup on pancakes. Carmen hated syrup—and pancakes.

"I'm Ashley, by the way," the girl said, extending her hand. "Domingo's girlfriend."

Girlfriend? Domingo's *girlfriend*? Carmen stared at the pretty young woman in disbelief. *Please*, Carmen implored silently, *someone put me out of my misery*.

"Next in line!" The pimply-faced boy behind the counter was gesturing impatiently at Carmen and her mother. Saved, Carmen thought as she walked forward to the counter.

"See you later, D.," she said over her shoulder, abbreviating his name in a way that she hoped sounded casual and so over it. Then, just to prove she was mature, she added, "Nice to meet you, Ashley."

"What would you like?" the attendant asked. And because she was fairly certain that *I would like my boyfriend back* was not the right answer, Carmen stood silently as her mother ordered a small popcorn, a Diet Coke, and a pack of Mike and Ike candy.

While Carmen wasn't the only girl turning on the waterworks during *I Love You, Too, Puppy*, she was pretty sure that she was the only one crying so hard that her mother had to get up, go to the bathroom, and return with an entire roll of toilet paper to mop up her tears. At one point, it got so bad that her mother actually told her to be quiet. But there was nothing Carmen could do. She was a wreck. And after a while, her mother simply took her hand and held it, the only comfort she could give in the quiet theater.

Of course Domingo had a girlfriend. That's what college was all about, Carmen thought between sobs.

Then she thought: *Why don't I have a boyfriend? It's Saturday night, and I'm at the movies with my mom. If that's not the definition of being a big loser, I do not know what is.*

When she felt as if she'd examined her pathetic, dateless existence as much as humanly possible, Carmen's thoughts turned back to Domingo's girlfriend. She was petite. Five foot one, at most. And she had one of those curvy Barbie-doll figures that Carmen had always envied. Domingo's girlfriend was a curvy Barbie munchkin. Was that why Carmen and he had broken up? Was she—Carmen—too tall? Too bony? Did Domingo have a thing for Barbie munchkins that she'd never known about?

It was all too sad for words. By the end of the movie, when the couple on the screen had a wedding with their puppies standing in as best man and maid of honor, Carmen was a sniveling, red-faced mess. *I'll be alone for the rest of my life*, she thought as she sobbed.

Domingo didn't even look as if he missed her. When she had first gone back to school and told everyone that she was fine about the breakup—after all, she had initiated it—she'd been lying. Of course she missed him a little bit. They'd dated for over a year. That meant something to her. Clearly—it was all so clear to her now—it had meant nothing to him.

"I'm so sorry, *niña*," her mother whispered as they walked out of the theater. "Let's take the south exit; it leads directly to the parking lot. We'll go right home."

Clutching the roll of toilet paper as if she were a five-year-old kid hanging on to her blankie, Carmen sniffed and docilely followed her mother.

And then, the evening that she thought couldn't get any worse got much, *much* worse.

In front of her very red, very swollen eyes, she saw Gaz, Alicia, Jamie, and Dash stumble out of another theater in the triplex. They were all so into each other and laughing so hard they didn't even notice Carmen at first. She stared at them, furious that they'd lied to her, and even more heartbroken than she had been just a moment before.

Just then, they saw her. Sheepishly, they walked over.

"Hey, Carmen, how's it going?" Gaz asked, giving her and her mom quick hugs.

Looking guilty and miserable, Alicia mumbled, "My parents' dinner finished early, so . . ."

Jamie, also looking as if she'd been caught in a lie, fumbled for an excuse. "We tried to call you, but . . ."

Carmen could feel the tightness in her voice, but she was too tired and sad to hide it. "Whatever. I'll see you guys in school on Monday."

Carmen held it together until she got into the car. The minute she strapped on her seat belt, she started to cry even harder than she had in the theater. Everything came down on her all at once. Domingo and his new girlfriend. Alicia and Jamie sneaking behind her back and leaving her out of going to a stupid movie, because she didn't have a boyfriend. Not to mention all the stress she'd been under with school, the formal, and the *quince* stuff.

Her mother tried a few times to get her to talk, but Carmen just cried. For the entire ride home, the only sound was the wind through the open window and the sniffling as Carmen failed to fight back the tears.

"How was the film?" her stepfather asked as Carmen and her mother entered the house. Then he saw Carmen's tear-stained face and the nearly empty toilet-paper roll that she clutched and said, "That bad, huh?"

"That bad," Carmen whispered. Then she climbed the stairs to her room.

Her phone, which she had left by the bed, was buzzing, and she picked it up. Twelve missed calls. All from Jamie and Alicia. Of course, there was nothing from Domingo. He'd moved on, and she hadn't. He was happily coupled, while she was going to be alone for the rest of her life.

Lying down, she curled up into a ball and wept.

CHAPTER 10

THE NEXT DAY, Carmen woke to find that the blackboard in the family kitchen was covered with messages:

> *Call Domingo.*
> *Jamie called.*
> *Call Alicia.*
> *Please call Alicia.*
> *Jamie says sorry.*
> *Domingo says call right away.*

It was Sunday, so her mother was doing her usual brunch spread, including Carmen's favorite, huevos rancheros.

"I didn't hear the phone ring," Carmen said, gesturing at the messages.

"Lucky you," her sister Una said snippily. "I've been

up since eight because of you and your phone-happy friends."

Carmen's little sisters, Lindsay and the twins, Laura and Lula, padded into the kitchen in matching footed pajamas.

"Car-men," Laura called out, breaking her name into distinct syllables the way she always did. "You promised you'd make astronaut suits for our Barbies."

"Yeah," Lula added. "They're flying to Mars *tonight*."

Carmen sighed, staring at the blackboard. Then she turned to her younger sisters. "Two astronaut suits, coming right up. They'll be ready in time for their space walk. But right now, I need to make a few phone calls."

She grabbed the house phone and took the stairs two at a time. For a loser dateless girl, she was feeling oddly energetic. Maybe this was the denial phase people talked about in the grieving process. She took the phone out to her favorite spot in the house, the little terrace that overlooked the canal. Christian called it the Juliet balcony.

Still in her gray and white pin-striped pj's, Carmen perched herself on the little wooden chair that overlooked the water and wondered whom to call first. She knew Alicia and Jamie were calling to apologize— and after a good night's sleep, and in the light of a new morning, she no longer felt the Shakespearean level of betrayal that she had felt the night before. She knew her friends were just trying to protect her. And judging by the way she'd cried like a baby during a movie about two talking dogs, clearly she needed more protecting than she had realized. Her friends would apologize for lying about going out, and she would forgive them . . . eventually.

Domingo was another matter entirely. She had no idea why he was calling. And the not knowing made her nervous. Carmen decided to call her *amigas* first. She dialed Jamie's number, and her friend picked up on the first ring.

"Carmencita! You okay, girl?" Jamie asked, her voice heavy with concern.

"Besides the fact that my two best friends lied to me in the same night? I'm cool," Carmen replied. Just because she'd woken up on the forgiving side of the bed didn't mean that her *amigas* shouldn't work for it, just a little. Some groveling was in order.

She could hear Jamie's voice sink. "About that—I'm sorry."

Carmen smiled slightly and said, "Sorry enough to help me find some fab Lucite bracelets on eBay to ensure your forgiveness?"

"Whatever it takes," Jamie said, laughing in relief.

"*Gracias, chiquita,*" Carmen said. She spent a few more minutes filling Jamie in on what had happened at the movies—and how crazy everyone in the theater must have thought she was—before saying good-bye and hanging up; everything was now back to normal.

Next she dialed Alicia. Leaning on the balcony railing, she watched a father with three little kids sail a yellow rowboat down the canal. The kids were screaming in delight, as if they were on the funniest roller coaster in the world. It reminded Carmen of when she, Una, and Tino were little and Christian had used to row them around. It wasn't so long ago that the Littles—Carmen's pet name for her three younger stepsisters—thought the rowboat was as big as the mammoth cruise ships that were docked all around Miami.

"*Hola,*" Carmen said, when Alicia finally picked up the phone.

Alicia launched into a terribly sweet monologue about how terrible she felt about hiding the double date. She didn't know whether Carmen would've felt better coming along without a boyfriend or whether, in the wake of Domingo, she preferred to see her *amigas* when they were sans their dudes.

Carmen shrugged. "It probably just depends on the day. But ask me next time. By lying to me, you didn't even give me a chance to choose."

Alicia's voice was thick with regret. "I know. I feel terrible. I'm sorry."

As she had done with Jamie, Carmen didn't immediately let her off the hook. "Sorry enough to ask Gaz if he would drive all the way to Pembroke Pines to pick up a special silver carpet runner that we're renting for the winter formal?"

"Of course," Alicia answered right away. "He's got the van, and I'll go with him. By the way, good job making me really work for this apology."

"It's how I roll," Carmen said playfully.

Alicia paused. "Seriously, though. How are you? I talked with Jamie briefly, and she said something about Domingo being there with another girl?"

Carmen sighed. "I was bad yesterday, but today, I'm pretty good."

"I'm glad, C.," Alicia said. "And while last night wasn't a great example, you know that the boys will come and go, but *amigas* are forever, right?"

"*Gracias*, A." They talked for a few more minutes, with Carmen giving directions to the store, and then hung up.

Those two calls had been easier than anticipated. As Alicia had said, Carmen knew her *amigas* were always there for her.

But the next call wasn't going to be so easy.

She hadn't spoken to Domingo in over two months, but she still knew the number by heart. Unfortunately, her fingers were shaking so hard that she dialed two wrong numbers before getting it right.

"Hello Domingo, it's Carmen," she said when she heard his voice on the other end of the line.

"Hey, what's the *qué pasa*?" he asked, casually and cheerfully, as if they were just two old friends catching up.

Carmen was confused. He had been so weird last night. And didn't he realize that this wasn't easy for her. What game was he playing? All she did know was that she didn't know what to think. Then she heard her mom's voice in her head. Whenever there was drama in their household—and with a Chicana mom, a British stepdad, and six kids under one roof, there was bound to be drama—her mother always said, "Why don't you try being honest? Honest works."

So, she took a deep breath and said, "Honestly, I'm just returning your call. And . . ."

Carmen was surprised by the little catch in her

voice and the way the emotions were still swirling around unsettled inside her.

She continued, "And I'm a little nervous, because last night was really awkward."

Carmen could hear Domingo exhaling on the other end of the line. He seemed relieved that she'd broached the topic. "That's why I called, C. It was awkward for me, too. I was hoping we could talk. Could I come over?"

Part of her really wanted to see him. Another part of her couldn't get the image of his hand, entwined with his new girlfriend's, out of her head. That was still fresh and painful, almost overpowering everything else. But talking to her girls had helped. Maybe it would help to talk to him, too. And if he came over to her house, she'd have home-court advantage. If she started to fall apart, she could retreat to her room. No worrying about walking through a movie-theater lobby and running into people. She told him to come over.

By the time Domingo rang the doorbell, two hours later, Carmen had changed out of her outfit five times and restyled her hair twice as many times as that. She was in the process of putting her long hair up in a pony-tail for the umpteenth time when she heard Christian call out, "Carmen, you've got company!"

She walked down the stairs and stopped for a nanosecond to catch a glimpse of herself in the mirror. She was wearing a long, tie-dyed yellow and white patio dress that she'd made herself, inspired by an old photo she'd seen of her mother in Mexico. She wore her favorite pair of sparkly flip-flops, and the ponytail, she hoped, conveyed a casual, not-trying-too-hard vibe.

Domingo stood in the kitchen sipping a glass of water. He looked more handsome than any ex-boyfriend had a right to be, and his outfit was one she'd never seen before: a brown and white checkered shirt, paint-splattered khakis, and brown, round-toed, leather work boots. He looked downtown and cool, like an artist in the Deco district.

Carmen pointed to his pants. "So, you paint now? Or did you buy them that way?"

Domingo looked down and laughed. "I paint now. First rule of art school: get off the computer and into the studio. Canvases before screens."

Carmen was intrigued. When she and Domingo dated, she had come to believe that he was actually surgically attached to his laptop. It was hard to imagine him as a junior Jackson Pollock when Carmen had always seen him as a Latino Bill Gates. "Wow. That's different." Carmen smiled, hoping that her voice didn't sound as sarcastic as she felt. "So, are you any good?"

Domingo shook his head. "Not even close. But as my teacher, Ms. Bevill, says, I'm bad in interesting ways."

Carmen laughed and took a seat at the kitchen counter, next to Domingo. Despite the butterflies in her belly, she was surprisingly calm now that he was there in her kitchen. It felt like old times. Almost.

"So, about last night . . ." Domingo began. "I'm sorry I didn't call you to let you know that I was back in town."

Carmen played nervously with the fringes of the napkin in front of her. "Ashley seems nice."

"She's great," Domingo said.

Carmen tried to keep herself from wincing.

"But Carmen," Domingo continued, "we've only been going out for a few weeks. And I guess what I wanted to say, why I came over, is that seeing you last night was confusing. If you think we should give this another chance . . ."

It was not what she had been expecting to hear. And she tried to figure out whether it was what she'd been hoping for. She and Domingo hadn't exchanged so much as an e-mail since he had left for college. They had both agreed that the best way not to hurt each other was by not being in touch. E-mails, they both felt, would end up becoming mysterious, postbreakup messages that would be hard to decode. But now Domingo had given her a signal that was not in the least bit mysterious. He wanted to try again . . . if she did.

Domingo got up and came over to stand behind her; he put his hands on her shoulders and began to massage them. He used to say that when she was tense, her shoulders touched her ears, that's how high and tight they'd get.

Now he was touching her in that way that made her feel good. Carmen relaxed; actually, she more than relaxed—she grew excited. She was ready for what came next. He kissed her—softly at first, then with more urgency. Even though they were standing in her family's kitchen, she felt completely swept away, as if she and Domingo were a movie-star couple kissing on the big screen. The dorky side of her—the sometimes shy, sometimes clumsy part—was sitting in the audience watching.

When they finally came up for air, Domingo looked at her hopefully. "Tell me that means yes."

Carmen couldn't believe how quickly her fortunes had shifted. Not even twenty-four hours before, she'd stood in that very same spot, crying her eyes out, her heart broken in a hundred pieces. It was as though the emotions had all been clouding her judgment, but now the sky had cleared. She was actually acutely aware of where she was, who she was, and what she wanted. She knew what she had to do.

"I love you, Domingo," she said. "I never loved anybody before you. You are my *first* love. But I think that your relationship with Ashley proves that our first love isn't the only love either of us is going to feel. I want you to have new adventures, that's what college is all about. It's *exciting* to see you in your paint-splattered pants, looking like a skinny Diego Rivera. But let's not be Frida and Diego. Let's not hurt each other by holding on when everything we know says we should let go. Who knows, maybe in a few years, when you're older and I'm wiser, we'll find our way back to each other."

Domingo took a step back. "Wow. That was either really deep or the nicest rejection any guy has ever gotten."

Carmen shrugged and smiled. "Did you like the Frida and Diego reference?"

Frida was Domingo's favorite movie. He and Carmen had watched it so many times Carmen had begun to suspect that Domingo cared less about the artist than the R-rated shots of Salma Hayek, the actress who played the influential Mexican painter.

"You're right," Domingo said. "I don't want to hurt each other like Diego and Frida. But I also don't think this is how *our* movie ends."

Carmen hugged him tight. "Well, then we'll both have to keep on watching. I like sequels."

He kissed her on the forehead. "I like sequels, too. And you know *Empire Strikes Back* is a much better movie than *Star Wars*."

"Meaning?" Carmen asked.

"Sometimes the sequel is better than the original," Domingo explained, looking handsome and earnest.

"I'll keep that in mind," Carmen said, running her hand along the back of his neck.

He turned to leave, and she walked him to the front door.

"'Bye, Domingo," she called out, as she watched him walk away. And for the first time, she was able to admit that she *would* miss him. She *had* missed him. But now she was just happy for him—and for herself.

When she stepped back into the kitchen, she was surprised to see that while they had been alone a moment ago, the room was now full. Her mother was making huevos rancheros. Christian was making lemonade. Tino was pouring potato chips into a bowl, because he was a teenage boy who ate like a pig. Una was on the phone, and Lindsay and the twins were drinking yogurt smoothies in the breakfast nook. The sight of her entire family, appearing out of nowhere, was startling.

"Carmen! Astronaut suits!" Lula called out.

"Where did you all come from?" she asked.

"Mom made us all go out to the garden so you and lover boy could have privacy," Tino teased.

"Yeah," Una added, rolling her eyes in mock annoyance. "Way to inconvenience the *entire* household."

Carmen walked over to her mother and gave her a big hug. "*Gracias, Mamacita,*" she said.

"Good talk?" her mother asked as she cracked an egg.

"Great talk," Carmen answered. She pulled up a chair next to her mother and was just about to tell her all about it when the twins ran over with their completely naked Barbie dolls.

"Car-men!" they cried out in unison. "Astronaut suits by dinner! You promised."

"I can do that," Carmen replied, breaking into a wide grin. "If I put my mind to it, I can do just about anything."

CHAPTER 11

CARMEN'S realization that she could do anything couldn't have come at a better time, because there was still plenty left to do when it came to the double *quinceañera*. One afternoon, the week after the Domingo run-in, Jamie entered the school gym. A few leftover Halloween decorations still dotted the walls of the gym, where the girls' basketball team was finishing up practice with an intersquad game. Taking a seat in the bleachers, she watched the action.

Patricia wasn't the tallest or the biggest girl on the team, but she was definitely the fastest. In the final minute of play, Patricia—her hair pulled back into a messy bun—stole the ball from a girl twice her size, dribbled quickly all the way down the court, and scored on a three-point jumper.

Even Jamie, who knew little about sports, knew that she had just witnessed something extraordinary.

She leapt to her feet and burst into applause. Patricia, hearing the sound, looked up into the bleachers and gave Jamie a thumbs-up.

After Patricia took what she assured Jamie was a much-needed shower, the two girls headed downtown to Joy Cards, the *amigas'* favorite stationery shop. It had been decided that various tasks would be handled by each *quince* separately, so that more could get done in a shorter amount of time. They just had to make sure that whatever they chose—whether stationery or dishes— would go with the theme and be appealing to both girls.

From the moment they arrived at Joy Cards and pushed the doors open to the tiny art studio, they felt as if they had been transported from their modern tropical city to an elegant little studio in London or Paris.

Joy Chen, who owned the shop, was a beautiful Cuban Chinese woman, who regularly topped the *amigas'* list of Who I Want to Be When I Grow Up. Today she was dressed in a crisp white shirt, a vintage silk silver mini, and bright red heels. She looked stunning.

"*Hola, Jamie, ¿qué tal?*" she said, kissing her favorite client on both cheeks.

Jamie introduced Patricia to Joy. Then the two girls followed Joy back through the rows of cards, candles, and other girlie gift items to an antique wooden table in the back room bedecked with a bowl of hot pink peonies. Joy offered each of the girls a cup of green tea, and as they held the delicate blue porcelain cups in their hands, Patricia giggled nervously. "This is so not me. I feel like a bull in a china shop. But I love it! Please don't make me leave."

Jamie smiled. "That's what we say every time we come here."

It was time to get down to work. Joy lay out binders of her custom-made card designs, all of which were unique and beautiful. But three cups of green tea later, while Patricia had seen lots of things she liked, there was nothing that she loved or that she thought Carolina would be okay with, too. Jamie was beginning to worry; everybody usually loved Joy's work.

But Joy wasn't fazed.

"I think the problem is that with a double *quince*, it's really hard to assert your individuality," Joy explained. "You need every element of this celebration to be specific to you, not generic. But you also want it to speak to your cousin's sensibilities as well. That is a lot to take on. But I think we can fix it. I'll be right back."

Joy returned with a portfolio of vintage magazine covers. "I use these for inspiration," she said, flipping the pages quickly, "and ever since you walked in, you have reminded me of one picture in particular."

She stopped on a page with a photo of Selena Gomez in the middle. The young actress's long dark hair was teased into a high ponytail and her eyes were fringed with fake lashes that were so thick they looked like birds' feathers, but other than the dramatic eyes, her makeup was soft, with just the sheerest hint of pink on her lips.

"Oh, my goodness, she's beautiful," Patricia said. "But I'm not sure I see the connection to my invitations."

"My thought is that we turn your invitation into a little pullout magazine, with covers of you and your cousin, the event details as the table of contents, and maybe some fun trivia pages about your lives written like magazine articles," Joy suggested.

Patricia grinned. "It's genius."

Joy took a seat beside the *quince* at the long wooden table. "Well, it wouldn't be cheap. We can do the photo shoot here at the studio. I have a friend who is a photographer. And I know Carmen and Jamie can handle the wardrobe and accessories. But we definitely need professional hair and makeup, because if the look isn't done exactly right, it'll be clownish. Plus, the interiors will have to be in color to make the minimagazine, and if you want two hundred invites, it'll be expensive. I'll have to send you an estimate, Jamie, when I really price things out."

Jamie nodded, then turned to Patricia. "I have an idea. Since this will run on the high end, why don't we make the invitation into your main party favor—a preparty favor sort of. We can do something really inexpensive for the real favor, maybe skipping bags altogether and juggling the budget in other little ways. But you should talk to Carolina to make sure she is cool with it, and then both of you should talk to your parents."

As the girls talked, Joy picked up the samples and stepped into the back room. She returned a few minutes later. "I made color copies for you and your cousin and for the Amigas team," she said, handing both Jamie and Patricia a small stack of papers. "Hopefully, it will help when you are filling your cousin and family in."

As they walked back toward the front door, Patricia turned to shake Joy's hand. "Really, really nice to meet you!" she said, brightly.

"You, too!" Joy said, cheerfully. "But I have to warn you, if you and your cousin don't go for my invite, I'll have to use this design for someone else. It's too good to waste!"

"I don't think that will happen," Patricia said gravely. "Trust me."

On the way to the bus stop, Patricia and Jamie passed Sweet and Tart, one of the city's hopping new cupcake shops. It was full of couples holding hands, cute boys drinking the store's already-famous chocolate espresso shots, and fashionable women in high heels and designer dresses who looked as if they might just as well have been sitting on a yacht as in a bakery. Jamie and Patricia peered in at the window.

"I know we just had three cups of tea," Jamie said, slowing down, "but I'm a sucker for this place's cucumber lemonade."

"And I'm a sucker for their butterscotch-caramel cupcakes; so we've got to stop in," Patricia agreed.

The girls found a table right by the window, a prime spot for people-watching. As the tanned and fashionable inhabitants of the neighborhood strolled in and out of the store, the two girls started in on their treats.

Halfway through her cupcake, Patricia paused in the middle of a bite. "Jamie," she said, her voice soft, "can you keep a secret?"

Jamie was intrigued. "*Claro que sí.*"

The other girl looked around the room, as though

making sure no one was listening or watching. "I have a crush," she finally said shyly. At Jamie's raised eyebrow, she added, "And you totally would never guess who the guy is."

Jamie was now doubly intrigued. While Carolina had had plenty of boyfriends and was usually romantically linked to someone if only by the rumor mill, Patricia tended to be focused on sports and her friends. Hearing that she had a crush was sort of surprising. "You *have* to tell me, because I'll never guess."

Patricia took a deep breath. "Jeff Giles."

Jamie nodded. "Captain of the football team. He's a jock, you're a jock. Why is that so odd?"

Taking another bite of her cupcake, Patricia shook her head. "That's not the way these things go. Guy athletes hardly ever date girl athletes. At least, not at C. G. High. They only date the four *P*'s: pretty, perfect, petite, preppy girls, like Carolina. That's why I decided to run for winter formal queen. I know it is totally insane, but I want—no, I *need*—for Jeff to see me as more than just another jock."

Jamie smiled. For a long time, she had believed that you could only date people who were similar to you, but after she met Dash, that opinion had changed. She could sympathize. "I get it," she said, nodding. "And since the queen gets to pick her king . . ." It was a winter formal tradition that a king wasn't chosen in the same way a queen was. In a sort of Sadie Hawkins twist, the queen picked her own king that night.

". . . What better, more magical time to let him know how I feel?" Patricia finished with a sigh. "I swear, it's all I think about."

Jamie held up a hand. "But Carolina and Jeff are friends, aren't they? I mean, I've seen them having lunch together and talking in the halls."

Patricia nodded.

"She's your cousin, your *prima hermana*," Jamie added. "So why don't you tell her the truth? That *Jeff* is the reason you're running for queen. She needs to know that you're not doing all of this just to steal her thunder."

Patricia shook her head. "That's the thing, though. The minute I mentioned wanting to run for winter formal queen, Carolina *completamente* lost it. She never even gave me a chance to explain. If she doesn't trust me enough to listen to me for five minutes about what being queen means to me, how am I supposed to trust *her* to tell her what's so deep in my heart?"

She had a point, Jamie thought. Growing up in the South Bronx, developing a style and having experiences that were worlds away from Alicia's and Carmen's, it had taken her a long time to trust her friends completely. But they had been there for her when she met Dash and had to work through the issues that came with dating a successful golf player who happened to be the son of one of the wealthiest industrialists in Miami. Alicia and Carmen had supported her—even when she flipped out on them. She was sure that Carolina would do the same if Patricia gave her the chance. But judging by the stubborn tilt of her chin, Patricia wasn't about to try. Not yet, anyway.

"Well," she said to Patricia, "I still think it would go a long way to tell her, but in the meantime, I can't stand in the way of a great crush. So you're just going to have to be elected queen. And I'm going to do my best to help without overstepping my Amigas boundaries."

Jamie got to work right away. She knew from her own painful past experiences that she had to be careful not to do anything that might jeopardize the harmony among the partners in Amigas Inc. or reflect badly upon their business. But still . . . she was competitive and liked a good challenge. She told herself that Carmen must be feeling the exact same way. After taking care of some more *quinceañera* business, she worked until after midnight on a new series of winter formal queen election posters. And early the next morning, she and Patricia met at school to hang them all up before the other students arrived.

The first bell of the morning rang just as the two girls finished. They were walking down the hallway, tired, but proud of the work they had done, when they were confronted by Carolina and Carmen, who were both irate.

"Nice work, Patricia," her cousin hissed. "You win the awards for most ginormous posters. Did you design them to match the size of your mouth?"

Patricia looked as if she'd been slapped. "What are you talking about, Caro?"

Carolina tried to speak, but she was so angry that she couldn't get the words out.

Carmen explained: "Eleven by seventeen is the size limit for all campaign posters. Attached to the wall by tape or tacks. What are your posters? Twenty-three by forty-five? I don't want to be a tattletale, but I will report you to the planning committee if necessary."

Jamie had been nervous about this happening. While she wanted to help Patricia on a personal level, as a friend, *both* of the girls were clients. They couldn't be fighting this much. It put everything in jeopardy.

"Look, this is my fault. I got inspired last night, and I went to town on the posters," said Jamie. "I had no idea there were size regulations. I'll make smaller posters tonight."

"Thanks, Jamie," Carmen said, sounding actually grateful, even though Carolina still looked livid. It was obvious she had been thinking the same thing and needed *everyone* calm . . . even if she was now sort of friends with Carolina.

Without another word, the two pairs turned in opposite directions and headed down the hall, toward their first classes.

By the next day, despite the temporary truce they had seemed to reach, both Patricia and Carolina had brand-new posters hanging in the halls.

Carolina's, which featured a red and hot pink fleur-de-lis pattern and gold stenciled letters, read:

CAROLINA'S SMART.
CAROLINA'S GREEN.
IF YOU LOVE THIS PLANET,
MAKE CAROLINA QUEEN.

Patricia's posters, which featured Jamie's famous graffiti-style print against a Miami skyline, read:

IF SKILLZ ARE WHAT YOU WANT,
PATRICIA'S GOT GAME.
IF YOU WANT TO SHAKE THINGS UP,
THEN PATRICIA IS THE NAME.

It didn't take long for the halls of C. G. High to start buzzing with whispers about the increased tension between the cousins. It was the school's own personal *telenovela*. Sides were clearly being drawn; Patricia's participation further confused matters, while disbelief was felt by many in the wake of Carolina's suddenly aggressive campaign style. All in all, the campaign was definitely shaking things up, and whether the *amigas* liked it or not, they were smack-dab in the middle of it.

It was time to put an end to the insanity. Or at least try.

After school, Patricia and Carolina met Alicia, Carmen, and Jamie in the library for a *quince* meeting. "Okay, guys, we really need to focus," Alicia began. "Put aside your fight for right now and think about your party. There is still a lot to do and just a few weeks left to do it. So, I had an idea. While each girl will have her court of *damas*, why don't we up the mystery quotient of the masked-ball theme and just not have any *chambelanes*?"

Patricia shook her head. "No dudes? No way!"

"I hate to say it, but Patricia's right," Carolina concurred. "We're not at an all-girls school; we've got to have guys."

"Hold up, hold up," Alicia interjected. "I didn't make myself clear. Of course there'll be guys at the *quince*. I'm not *loca*."

She then explained that, starting in the nineteenth century at masked balls in Venice, women carried intricately decorated dance cards, which men would sign. At the Reinosos' *quince*, they would take this tradition and spin it. The entire ball would be a ladies' choice, with *guys* carrying the dance cards and girls picking the boys they wanted to partner with for each dance. If either cousin had a favorite, she could fill up his entire dance card. If not, she could play the field, embracing the fact that as a young woman, she could make her own decisions.

When she was done explaining, all the girls looked impressed.

"I like it," Patricia said finally, with a firm nod.

"I *love it*," Carolina said, enthusiastically.

"Me, too," added Carmen.

"It's *fresh*," Jamie noted, bestowing her highest compliment on the idea.

Jamie pulled up an image of an old-fashioned dance card on her iPhone and showed it to the group. "I love it. But here's a thought: what if I design the cards to have fifteen dances, and whoever you each choose to dance the fifteenth dance with is your *chambelán* of honor?"

"It's genius," Patricia and Carolina crooned simultaneously. For the first time in a long time, they entirely agreed on something: without a doubt, their *quince* was going to be the most elegant, most intriguing ball the town had ever seen. Now, if only the two cousins could get to the big night without scratching each other's eyes out.

CHAPTER 12

THE NEXT MORNING, all of the juniors were called into the auditorium for assembly. Alicia and Carmen walked in together. Alicia was wearing a denim bustier, black silk harem pants, and platform shoes that were hand-me-downs from her superstylish mom. Carmen was dressed in one of her own creations—a white halter-topped jumpsuit with a fitted dark denim blazer over it.

"How much do I love assembly?" Alicia asked. "If this goes long enough, I'll not only miss Russian lit, but part of AP biology, too."

Carmen looked surprised. "Come on, Lici, you're Miss four-point-oh GPA. I would think you would hate skipping classes."

As the students rushed in and filled the auditorium, Alicia pouted. "I know. I know. When it comes to the GPA, I'm rocking it. But if one more teacher says, 'Fun and games are over. Every grade counts for your college application now,' I'm going to scream! I don't want the fun and games to be over. We spent so much of sophomore year juggling school and building up Amigas Inc. I feel like the fun is just starting."

"Hey, Alicia," Gaz called out. Tanned and handsome in an ocean blue button-down, he gestured toward the seats next to him.

Carmen followed her friend over to him. But by the time they got there, there was only one seat available.

Carmen pushed Alicia toward it. "Sit with your boyfriend, *chica.*"

Alicia looked uncertain. "I don't want you to go solo."

Carmen laughed. "It's only an assembly." She'd survive. And she would. Ever since her talk with her ex, she had been fine about the Domingo situation. He was away at college. She had just turned sixteen. It'd be fun to be single for a little while.

Walking toward the back of the auditorium, she scanned the rows, looking for a place to sit. There was Jamie, seated with the new art teacher, Ms. Bagley. The two of them looked to be involved in an intense discussion. Carmen guessed it was probably about something unbelievably old-school and esoteric, like

Michelangelo or Gustav Klimt. While Jamie liked to play the hood card, the longer her friends knew her, the more it became apparent that she was equal parts South Bronx tough girl and art nerd. They'd made that discovery when the whole crew had gone to New York after Carmen's *quince* for a visit and Jamie had insisted on making their first priority a trip to the Metropolitan Museum of Art. Five hours after entering, they were all ready to gouge their eyes out, but Jamie was just getting started.

Carmen was still looking for a seat when she heard her name called. "Carmen, sit with us!" Even before she turned around, she knew it was Dorinda and the SoBees. She tried to pretend she hadn't heard them and kept looking. She could hear the principal, Mrs. Richards, addressing the room. "Everyone, please take a seat," she said, her voice booming over the microphone. "It's not a school dance. It's assembly. If you're separated from your friends, rest assured, they'll be waiting for you at lunchtime in your prearranged meeting places."

Then another voice called her name. "Carmen, over here!" She looked and saw that Carolina, in the middle of the center section, was gesturing to her.

Despite the fact that this meant squeezing past a

dozen annoyed classmates, Carmen shimmied down the row and took the seat next to Carolina.

"Thanks," Carmen whispered. "You saved me from the SoBees."

Carolina smiled. "Glad I could help." Then she gestured to the cute boy sitting next to her and whispered, "Do you know Maxo? He's the brains behind Blue and Green."

Maxo looked embarrassed. "Well, that's not true. But if I'm the brains, Carolina is the heart. She really cares about the environment."

Maxo was Haitian American; he had cocoa brown skin and a short curly Afro. While Mrs. Richards went on and on about the dos and don'ts of using personal electronic devices in school, Carmen answered texts from Alicia and stole glances at Maxo. He was supercute and seemed supersmart. She wondered why she hadn't noticed him before. But then she remembered that she'd been focused on Domingo. And it didn't matter anyway, as clearly, having an interest in him was out of the question, since he and Carolina seemed to be an item. Their foreheads almost touched as they whispered excitedly about carbon footprints, roof gardens, and how cool it would be if all of the school's floors were done in sustainable bamboo.

As the assembly dragged on, Carmen came to a rather startling revelation.

True, she had been honest with her friends when she told them she didn't feel the slightest pang when she saw Jamie with Dash or Alicia with Gaz. But she sincerely hoped that her new *amiga* and client didn't ask her to hang out with her often, because every time Carmen looked at Maxo, pangs were all she felt. It seemed that somewhere between sitting down and now, Carmen had developed a serious crush.

After the assembly was over, Carmen gave Carolina a quick hug. "So, we're meeting tonight about your *quince*, right?"

"Yep," Carolina replied. "At Las Ramblas. See you at seven."

"Nice to meet you, Maxo," Carmen said, trying to sound casual.

"The pleasure was all mine," he said, holding her hand as if he were a character in an old-fashioned movie—as if he might kiss it. "May we walk you to your class? What way you headed?"

Carmen could feel her knees buckling. *May we walk you to your class?* Wow! He was such a gentleman! How nice of him to be so concerned about the earth, because he was clearly from another planet. No boys she knew, not even Domingo, were this polite.

"I'm going over to the Humanities floor: Latin American lit," Carmen answered.

"How unfortunate," Maxo replied. "Carolina and I have oceanography. And . . ."

Carolina looked at her watch. "And it's all the way over in the annex. We're going to be late if we don't hurry."

Carmen waved good-bye and then walked slowly down the hall. She felt as if she were in one of those music videos where the girl singer is standing on a corner in New York City and all the people around her are moving so fast that they seem to be just flashes of light. Fast-moving balls of light: that was what all the students looked like to her as she walked down the hall. It was as though Carmen had been hit and pushed out of orbit. All because she had just met this guy—this *obviously* taken guy—and he had held her hand.

She had to fight the urge not to break out into a cheesy love song, not to start humming a Leona Lewis tune or something by Miranda Cosgrove.

Suddenly, she felt an arm on her shoulder, and she jumped, startled. Turning, she saw that it was Jamie. They had Latin American lit together.

"Didn't you hear me call you, *chica*?" Jamie asked.

Carmen shook her head.

Jamie looked at her quizzically. "You have the strangest expression on your face. What's the *qué pasa*?"

Carmen smiled. "I was just thinking that I might start singing a song."

Her friend sighed. "Like I said, strange. Why don't you sing us an excuse for the principal's office? Because the bell rang five minutes ago. And you know Señora Gonzalez won't let us into class without a late pass."

But even the stern lecture she got from Señora Gonzalez upon entering the class late couldn't burst the happiness bubble in Carmen's heart. All afternoon, she kept thinking about Maxo. That morning, when she'd gotten out of bed, she hadn't even known he existed. But now, he was in her thoughts . . . for better or worse.

CHAPTER 13

THAT SATURDAY, Carolina and Carmen met in order to shop for the material needed for the *quince* dresses. For Carolina, it was an adventure—traveling to Miami's design district, where bargain prices reigned, on everything from buttons to bed frames. The district was well known to the city's interior designers and retailers, but most high school students never had any reason to enter the big warehouselike buildings that stood in this part of the city.

For Carmen, visiting the big fabric shops and those who worked in them was like going to see members of her extended family. The women who ran the shops thought of themselves as the up-and-coming designers' fairy godmothers, and they insisted that the girls call them *tías*.

The girls began with Carmen's favorite, a sprawling space called Ceci's Fabrics. The owner, Cecilia

Noriega, was from Panama and referred to Carmen as her "honorary goddaughter."

"*Hola, Tía* Ceci," Carmen called out as they entered the store.

"*¡Mira, como te ves! ¡Más flaca cada vez!*" Ceci said, insisting, as she always did, that Carmen was too thin. "Don't starve yourself, *chica*. You're an original. You set fashion, don't follow it."

"Believe me, *Tía* Ceci," Carmen insisted. "I eat. I eat *a lot.*"

Dressed in a light gray pantsuit, Ceci charged through the store as if she were leading a presidential motorcade down Pennsylvania Avenue in Washington, DC. "What can I do for you?"

"I'm designing a dress for Carolina and her *prima hermana*," Carmen explained as she tried to keep up. "They're having a double *quince.*"

Ceci turned and smiled. "A double *quince. Qué bendición.* What a blessing. Because you are working with this gem of a designer, I'll give you an early birthday present. Twenty percent off any fabric you choose."

Carolina's eyes widened. "Wow, thanks."

"*De nada, niña, de nada,*" Ceci said. "I will leave you in the capable hands of Alma, who's been working with me for twenty years. *Trátale bien*, Alma. You know Carmen's my favorite."

Carmen hugged the store owner, then turned to the fabrics in the formal-wear section of the store.

"I know we said we'd go for a big Marie Antoinette hoop number for your dress, but I don't want it to look too costumey," Carmen explained. "I want to go for something soft, structural, and modern, like twenty-first-century pop queen meets eighteenth-century French queen."

Carolina laughed. "I have no idea what you're talking about, but I trust you. I know it'll be gorgeous."

Carmen walked through the store rejecting satins, taffetas, and lamés with a flick of her wrist. Finally, she settled on a bolt of silk fabric that started out white, then turned into a pale pink halfway through, getting darker and darker until the bottom layer of the bolt was a dark cherry pink.

Carmen and Carolina watched the saleswoman lay out yards of the hand-dyed fabric. Carmen touched it and urged Carolina to follow her lead.

"It's impeccable," Carmen commented approvingly. "What do you think?"

"Fabulous," Carolina agreed, smiling.

"Great! I'll come back with Patricia on Monday to

see what she'd like, but I don't think your dresses have to match," said Carmen. "It would better if they just echoed each other in an interesting way."

"Again, I don't completely get what you're saying," Carolina said, "but I trust you! The dresses will be amazing, I know it."

A few minutes later, fabric in hand, the two girls walked down the sunny Miami street; the palm trees along the sidewalks provided some welcome shade.

"Okay, that was easy!" Carmen said. "Now for the tougher stuff. I need to go across town to pick up a snow machine for the winter formal. Want to come along?"

Carolina stole a glance at her phone. "As exciting an offer as that is, since I have some extra time, I think I'll pop by the Blue and Green office."

Carmen's heart immediately began to race. She had tried to forget Maxo. Tried to pretend he didn't cause her knees to go weak or her pulse to race. She *had* to forget, because he wasn't hers to lust after. So she did what she usually did when she had no idea about how to handle something. She went for the light and breezy. "Going to see your boyfriend, Maxo?"

Carolina turned and cocked her head; there was a confused expression on her face. "Maxo?" she repeated. "Maxo's not my boyfriend. I'm crushing on Jean-Luc, the French exchange student. It's totally hopeless, but—"

The sound of the other girl's voice faded as Carmen's heart went from a jog to full-on sprint. This was news. Big news. If Maxo wasn't Carolina's boyfriend, then . . . then what? She didn't know, but she *really* wanted to find out.

"So, you'll be filling up Jean-Luc's dance card at your *quince*, huh?" Carmen asked, returning to the conversation. "If you want, we'll make sure no one else gets a single dance with him. It's the *quince* girl's prerogative to dance with whomever she likes."

Carolina shook her head. "Jean-Luc won't be coming to my *quince*."

"Is he going back to France early?" Carmen asked, confused.

"Nope," Carolina said. "He's here for the entire year. And I know for a fact that his parents are coming to Miami for Christmas."

"So, what's the problem?" Carmen wondered.

"Have you seen him?" Carolina asked.

Carmen nodded. She had. "He's cute. Supercute. In that sort of James Dean way."

"Exactly," Carolina said. "Let me explain something about my favorite Frenchman. He lives in a pair of skinny black jeans. I'm not entirely sure that he doesn't wear the same pair every day. He wears a black leather jacket unless it's above eighty degrees, and he's always in a pair of scruffy motorcycle boots. And, oh, yeah, did I mention that he actually rides a motorcycle, as well as a scooter, to school? A baby blue Vespa that his parents sent over from Paris. He doesn't like the beach. He doesn't like school dances. He doesn't like fluffy. In fact, I'm pretty sure he scoffs at girlie-girls. His only passion is the environment, which is what we have in common. The *only* thing we have in common. I'm the type of girl he wouldn't even look at twice if not for that. So, I can't very well have him see me in a big, frothy dress with girlie invites and whatnot. He would never believe I'm an eco-warrior. It would be over before it could even start."

Carmen wagged her finger and pretended to be offended. "First of all, I'm making your dress. So, trust. It will be fierce, not frothy. Second of all, lighten up a little bit, *chica*! The *quince* is your *birthday party*. And I'm fairly confident that people celebrate their birthdays in France. And third, you have to give yourself more credit. You are pretty fantastic, and he probably knows that. I mean, you can be girlie and a save-the-world type at the same time. There is no rule against that.

"Just like there is no rule that just because you dress all in black, you can't act green. *¿Comprendes?*" said Carmen. Quickly kissing Carolina on the cheek, she added, "I've got to run to a meeting with the SoBees, but my advice, *chica*? Go for it."

Walking away, she had to wonder if maybe, when it came to Maxo, she should take her own advice.

A few hours later, Jamie was working on special hand-made papier-mâché masquerade masks for Patricia and Carolina when she heard frantic knocking on her studio door. She opened it to see Carmen, who was completely freaking out.

"Can you make snow?" Carmen asked, the words coming out in a rush. "Because it's not a winter formal without real snow. And the SoBees neglected to tell me that if I didn't rent a snow-making machine by November first, I was bound to be out of luck. And the only one I can get is a model that has to be special-ordered from New York and, oh, yeah, it's five hundred dollars more than our budget allows." She finally stopped and took a breath.

Plopping down on the old couch in Jamie's studio, she added, "Can I move in here? It's nice here. I can hide out from the entire world and never have to worry about things like *quinces* and snow machines and winter formal queens."

"But you'd have to worry about me," Jamie reminded her. "And I'd have to kick you out because this is my studio, not a flop pad for my friends, no matter how much I love you. So how about another solution. Why don't you hold a bake sale to raise the money for the snow machine. Or, better yet, a car wash. All the parents who have filthy cars will come, and they tip really well; on a sunny Saturday afternoon, you could make five hundred dollars easy."

Carmen sat up, encouraged. "Hey, that's not a bad idea. Maybe Carolina has some green ideas for a car wash."

Not wanting to waste any time, Carmen texted Carolina, who wrote back right away: *Go see Maxo. He's a genius.*

Carmen let out a little whoop and stood up. This was a very good development. Very good indeed. She gave Jamie a little hug. "You are the best friend in the whole entire world."

Jamie raised an eyebrow. "Because I suggested you have a car wash?"

"Something like that," Carmen answered, closing the studio door behind her. Walking through the Sosa family's backyard, which was full of wildflowers and eucalyptus trees, it was all that Carmen could do not to sing a little. She hadn't wanted there to be a disaster with renting the snow machine. Honest to goodness, she wanted things to go smoothly. But a year of planning *quinces* had taught her that whenever you planned a huge party, there was bound to be at least one disaster. And she couldn't help but think how lucky it was that her disaster had a solution that led her right to Maxo.

CHAPTER 14

THE FOLLOWING Monday morning at school, Carmen was relieved to see that Carolina and Patricia seemed to be back on good terms. They were at their lockers, which were right next to each other, laughing and comparing notes about their *quince* dresses. Carmen was tempted to ask what had led to this change, but she decided to leave well enough alone. After all, wasn't the saying, basically, why fix what wasn't broken? Catching Carmen's eye, Carolina held up a swatch of her dress fabric for Carmen to see. "I slept with it underneath my pillow last night," she called out. "*Me encanta* this material."

Patricia laughed and added, "Don't forget we're picking out my dress today after school. I need to find something just as fab. I'll meet you in the quad."

Carmen smiled and waved. "*¡Claro!* See you then."

There was no way on earth that she could forget

about her meeting with Patricia, because she was scheduled within an inch of her life—or at least that's what it felt like these days. She'd set her phone with so many alarms and reminders that, the day before, the minute she got home, her sister Una growled, "Leave the demon phone in the kitchen. Last night, it woke me up at two a.m. When I looked at the message, it said, *Reminder: Brush your teeth.* Just because you're going *loca*, doesn't mean you have to drag the rest of the world down with you." While normally Carmen would have liked to argue that her sister was being way too melodramatic, in this case, she was right.

Now at least she was on the school schedule, which actually was a welcome relief. At least someone else had planned that! She was about to race down the hall to her next class, when out of the corner of her eye she noticed that the SoBees had gathered around Patricia's and Carolina's lockers.

"Your invite arrived last night. Totally cool," observed Maya.

"Def," April said. "I'm so excited about your *quince*. A masked ball is just so, so chic. My father ordered my dress from New York. It's a designer original."

"That's totally *haute*," Dorinda added, approvingly. "Of course, my dress is vintage couture. They're red-carpet veterans. I will be bringing it to the masked ball."

"Yeah, well, my dress is a Carmen Ramirez-Ruben original," Carolina said, holding up a swatch of material. "She's young, she's fresh, and you can't buy her dresses in stores. So, I've got you all beat. While you were out shopping, we've been busy *creating*."

Patricia gave her cousin a high five as Carmen walked down the hall, with a smile on her face that was bigger than Biscayne Bay. Not only had Carolina given her some crazy, unsolicited praise, but the Reinosos' joint fifteenth birthday and *quince* bash was turning into what Amigas Inc. desired for every *quince* they threw: that it be more than a party, that it be something closer to a real cultural event.

The SoBees walked away, debating among themselves as to whether Carolina's one-of-a-kind dress (albeit one made by a classmate) trumped one from a big-name designer. Just then, Jeff Giles, the sandy blond football star whom Patricia was crushing on, stopped in front of Carolina's locker.

"I got the invitation to your *quince*," he said, his voice deep as he locked eyes with Carolina. "Sounds pretty cool. Make sure you save a dance for me."

"I'm the *quinceañera*," Carolina said, her tone light and friendly. "All I've got to make sure to do is be beautiful and have fun."

Jeff looked as though he appreciated Carolina's bravado. "So, it's like that?" he asked playfully.

Carolina gave him a light punch on the shoulder, the way she did with all her buddies. She knew Jeff. He hung in the same circles, but she had always thought that he would be good with Patricia. "What it is, is a double *quince*, so I think you should make sure to dance with my cousin."

He gave Patricia the briefest of glances and shrugged. "I'll think about it. See you later."

As Jeff walked away, Patricia slammed her locker door, loud enough that Carolina could tell something was wrong.

"Are you okay, *prima*?" Carolina asked.

"Yeah, just fine," Patricia grumbled. Then she turned and rushed off to class, trying to hide the hurt in her eyes and the tears that threatened to spill over. That had been one of the most embarrassing moments of her life. She could only imagine what the party would be like.

As she watched her cousin run away, Carolina felt a chill. She had done something wrong. But what?

Later, she thought, when she could get a private moment with all of the Amigas—because she knew she was going to need the wisdom of all three wise *chicas*—she would ask what was up. Was there something about turning fifteen that made a girl lose her mind? Because ever since they started the countdown to the *quince*, Patricia had been anything but cool. And Carolina was getting sick of it. Things were crazy stressful for her, too. She needed her *prima hermana*. She missed her best friend.

The next day, Patricia was back on the warpath. The incident with Jeff had really rattled her, and after stewing over it all night long, she decided that she had to intensify her efforts to win the winter formal crown and show him that she, too, was worthy of his attention. To that end she set up a huge table in the school entryway with a sign that said: PATRICIA'S YOUR QUEEN BECAUSE SHE BRINGS THE HEAT!

When Carolina, Carmen, and Alicia approached the table, they saw that in addition to handing out campaign buttons, she was also passing out tickets to the next Miami Heat game.

Carolina's eyes grew wide. She loved her *prima*, but she had had it with Patricia.

Apparently, Carmen agreed. "You can't give out Miami Heat tickets!" she said. "That's not campaigning, that's *bribery!*"

Alicia nodded. "Come on, Patricia. This is way above the spending limit for a queen campaign."

But Patricia was defiant. "*Numero uno,* you guys aren't the boss of me. *Numero dos,* since my *papi*'s law firm represents the Heat, I got the tickets for free. And *numero tres,* I can share said free tickets with my friends and classmates if I want to."

The two *amigas* exchanged worried glances. They were used to dealing with *quince*-zillas. They knew the meltdowns that occurred when either a girl hated her dress, or when there were a hundred relatives flying in from the Dominican Republic, or when the birthday girl's family loathed her beloved *chambelán*. They were experienced in these delicate matters and had handled them all with grace and care. But the on-and-off war between the Reinoso cousins, highlighted by the fight for the winter formal queen title that just coincidentally overlapped with the lead-up to their *quince*, was brand-new territory; they really wished someone would toss them a road map. But until a *quince* fairy dropped an instruction manual in their lap, they were on their own.

Carmen tried to reason with Patricia. "Regardless of whether they were free, there's a line from here to the beach filled with C.G. kids waiting to get their Heat tickets, and I have to say that as a member of the winter formal committee, I'd consider this a form of bribery."

Patricia smiled sweetly, but her tone was icy when she replied. "Well, report me, and let the principal decide."

Up to that point, Carolina hadn't said anything. She had just stood there, eyes wide, her emotions running from hot to cold and back to burning. But now she spoke, her voice full of sadness and resignation. "This has gone too far. I can't have a *quince* with her. The party is off."

By lunchtime, the entire school was aware of the renewed conflict between the cousins; it seemed as though everyone had taken sides. And in the strangest twist of all, the SoBees decided that Patricia was the girl to back. Apparently, they had been very impressed by the ticket stunt.

"I told my dad that if we can't go to Cabo for Christmas, then we might as well stay home," the Amigas overheard Patricia saying from the SoBees' table a few feet away.

"Oh, Cabo sounds nice," said Dorinda.

"And warm," April whined as she ate tiny spoonfuls of frozen yogurt. "For whatever reason, my father insists we go to Vail for Christmas every year. I'm a black-diamond-level skier, I admit, but I look much cuter in a bikini than I do in a parka."

The SoBees all giggled in their usual *look at us, we're laughing* way, but it was particularly dispiriting to see Patricia chuckling right alongside them.

Things had gone from bad to worse . . . much, *much* worse.

That evening, Alicia, Carmen, and Jamie met to discuss how to save the joint Reinoso *quince*. They gathered at their favorite thinking spot—Alicia's family pool. Each girl sat perched on a beach towel at the pool's edge, bare feet dangling in the water.

"It's not just the *quince*," Carmen said. "These are two cousins who really love each other, and yet they are at each other's throats."

"So, how do we get them to work it out?" Alicia asked.

"I have no idea," Jamie shrugged. "I mean, really? All this drama about being winter formal queen . . . Am I the only one who's seen that wicked scary seventies movie *Carrie*, about the girl with telekinetic powers who wipes out her entire senior class on prom night?"

"I think it is about a lot more than the crown," Carmen said softly. "They are smart girls; there has to be something they aren't telling each other. Something that maybe is big enough to cause all this craziness."

Jamie was silent, her thoughts going back to Patricia's crush confession. She had promised not to say anything, but . . .

Two hours, a pitcher of *agua fresca*, and a plate of empanadas later, the girls still hadn't figured out a solution to the problem.

Just then, Gaz opened the patio door and walked out to the pool. His dark hair kept falling over and covering his eyes, but it made him look handsome and alluring.

He looked at the girls lounging poolside and laughed. "Hard at work, as usual." His remark was met with three splashes, and he threw up his hands and retreated to the patio table.

"So, *chicas*, fill me in," he said, to put a stop to the attack.

Alicia explained the situation.

Gaz listened carefully; he was always good at

listening, even when the topic was extra girlie—like *quince* drama. Then he said, "You can't fire your family. Put them in a room until they're ready to talk it out and work it out."

Alicia stood up, gave him a big hug and a kiss on the forehead, and said, "You are a genius. But you do know what your brilliance means, right?"

Gaz sighed. "It means you're canceling our date tonight."

"Not canceling," Alicia insisted. "Postponing. We'll go out tomorrow. I'll treat. But I really think I've got to deal with this situation now, before it gets even more out of hand."

Gaz hugged Alicia close as she walked him to the front door. Watching them leave, Carmen allowed herself to feel a pang for the time when she had had a steady boyfriend and she, too, had known the easy comfort of a boy's embrace. Then she thought of Maxo and wondered how he kissed. And how he hugged. Then she shook her head. She had to focus. They had an intervention to plan.

The girls got to work immediately. Jamie called Patricia and asked her to come over to Alicia's. Carmen called Carolina and asked her to do the same thing.

Twenty minutes later, Carolina arrived.

Patricia rang the bell seconds later. "What is she doing here?" she asked, indignantly.

"Come on, P.," Carolina said. "You're not this girl. Just stop, already."

"Oh, just like I'm not the girl who should be winter formal queen," Patricia snapped.

Carmen raised a hand, her expression stern. "Enough about winter formal queen!"

Alicia led the two girls to her family's Florida room, and using Gaz's words, she told them, "Try as you might, you can't fire family."

She settled them at a mahogany coffee table with a pitcher of virgin *mojitos* and urged them to work it out.

For the first twenty minutes, there was nothing but silence. Then Carolina and Patricia started yelling at each other, really getting into it. The *amigas*, listening from the other side of the door in the kitchen, wondered more than once whether they should step in and break it up.

But eventually, the screams died down, and then some soft mumbling could be heard, as Patricia and Carolina seemed to come clean about how each had always envied the other's gifts and abilities.

"You've always been the golden girl in the family,"

Patricia pointed out. "Everybody adores you."

They heard Carolina guffaw. "Yeah, right. I'm the worker bee! Gotta work at my hair. Gotta work at my skin. Gotta work at my grades. You're the natural talent. You're just naturally awesome."

"Well, now that you've flattered me . . ." Patricia responded. The three *amigas* heard the sound of a drink being poured.

"I'll tell you my secret, and why I've been so off the wall and obsessed," Patricia said. "I have a crush on Jeff Giles. I know he's the football star and you're the super-cute preppy girl, and you two belong together, but I adore him. I thought it if I were queen, he might see me differently."

Carolina nodded, a serious expression on her face. "Well, that's unfortunate."

Patricia's dark eyes flashed, and she looked as if she were going to snap again.

Carolina laughed. "I'm kidding, I'm kidding. I don't like Jeff. Jeff is a friend. A buddy. I like Jean-Luc."

"The French exchange student?"

Carolina nodded.

"Does he know?" Patricia asked, incredulous.

Carolina shook her head no.

"Well, we're a sorry pair," said Patricia with a sigh.

"Young, gifted, Latina, and completely unable to let two high school boys in on the fact that we're crushing on them. But willing to hurt each other in the process. What were we thinking? Boys should never come before friends or family!"

"We'll be okay, right?" Carolina added, giving her *prima* a hug.

"We'll be better than okay," Patricia said, returning the embrace. "We're great. And you know what? I think I have just the plan to make this whole queen thing work—for both of us!"

CHAPTER 15

FINALLY, it was the week before winter formal. Adding to the stress on Carmen, it was also Spirit Week at C. G. High. Along with Jamie and Alicia, Carmen helped the Reinoso cousins unleash a new campaign that sent the whole school into a fervor.

The new campaign featured posters that stated:

2 queens are better than one!
Vote for Patricia AND Carolina
for winter formal queen!

Alongside a supercute picture of both girls was written the following: WHO WILL BE OUR KINGS?

And just to show that there was no more competition between these *primas hermanas,* Carolina put one of the posters next to Jeff Giles's locker and slipped a note inside the locker that said, *Don't you think my prima is cute?* She made sure to sign it so Jeff wouldn't be confused.

Unbeknownst to her, at the very same time, Patricia was putting a poster on the wall right near Jean-Luc's locker. When Jean-Luc walked by, Patricia yanked his arm and asked, "How do you say *beautiful* in French?"

Jean-Luc, dressed in his uniform of black leather jacket and jeans, looked amused. "*Belle*," he responded.

Patricia smiled. "That's like Spanish. In Spanish, we say *bella*. And how do you say *cousin*?"

Jean-Luc paused and said, "Depends. Are we speaking about a male or a female?"

Patricia jerked her thumb toward the poster. "We're talking about her. My cousin Carolina."

Jean-Luc laughed as he realized what Patricia was trying to tell him. "For a female, we say *ma cousine*."

"See, that's crazy," Patricia said. "People are always saying French is harder than Spanish. But French is easy. So, listen up, Frenchie. *Ma cousine* is *belle*. And if I were you, I wouldn't sleep on that. Got it?"

Jean-Luc nodded obediently. "Got it. You're having a birthday party, yes? What do you think Carolina would like as a birthday present?"

Patricia smiled. "What she would like is to dance with you all night long. But you did *not* hear that from me."

She took off down the hall, but not before she gave Jean-Luc one more glance. He was awfully cute. When they were in junior high, Carolina and Patricia had loved to watch the Pirates of the Caribbean movies on DVD. Jean-Luc looked like the child of Orlando Bloom and Keira Knightley. She had to admit her cousin had good taste in guys.

Argh, she thought as she took off down the hall. *Jeff Giles doesn't even know I exist, and my* prima *is about to have a storybook romance with the* más *que caliente French guy. The things I do for family.*

The Amigas and the Reinoso *primas* were hanging out on the front steps of C. G. High later that day when they were approached by the SoBees.

Even though Carmen had gotten them to do a little work for the winter formal, the SoBees still found the rich-and-spoiled routine pretty hard to shake. And despite the fact that the socialites of C. G. High not only had all the money in the world and a *Project Runway* level of fashion knowledge, they still insisted on dressing alike. Today's uniform was a sherbet-colored cashmere sweater, identical miniskirts, multicolored designer handbags, and candy-colored platform heels. Dorinda was dressed in a red mini, April was dressed in a pink one, and Maya was dressed in orange.

"Toodles," they announced in unison.

"What you are attempting to do is *so* not cool," Maya protested. "The quest for winter formal queen is a serious competition, like *American Idol*. It's not some lovey-dovey Girl Scout routine where we all hold hands and sing 'Kumbaya.'"

"Exactly," April said. Her lipstick matched her crimson sweater. "There's got to be a winner, and there's got to be a loser."

Dorinda added, "Patricia, we backed you because we thought you had some fight. Maybe we were wrong."

Patricia shook her head. "No, you guys backed me because you thought that I was willing to do whatever it takes, and spend however much it cost, to be queen. Which I'm not."

"Exactly," Carolina said, throwing her arm around her *prima*'s shoulder. "We want to use Spirit Week to lift spirits, not crush them."

The SoBees looked categorically unimpressed.

"What-evs," Dorinda said, snapping her fingers.

"You'll regret this. I promise you." She teetered away in her sky-high heels. April and Maya followed right behind.

"I'm so proud of you both," Carmen said when they were gone, turning to give the Reinoso girls a hug.

"Me, too," Jamie added.

"Me, *tres*," Alicia chimed in.

But a whole new can of worms had been opened. They just didn't know it.

By homeroom the next morning, the school's hallways were covered with posters announcing the latest crown-drama participant: Dorinda. There were tables set up with cupcakes that had Dorinda's picture on them, and freshman girls stood in the hallway passing out Dorinda Dollars, which were good for discounts at all the restaurants within walking distance of C. G. High. Carmen wondered how the SoBees had time to mount such an elaborate campaign in less than twenty-four hours yet couldn't lift a finger to help with the formal. It was actually kind of impressive.

The posters featured a photo of Dorinda sporting a silver tiara and sitting behind the wheel of one of her father's powder blue Mercedes convertibles. Largely because of the flashy car, the pictures were attracting a huge amount of attention from the students—both girls and boys. The girls debated Dorinda's worthiness to be queen. The boys were all geeked out about her wheels. Dorinda's campaign slogan wasn't the best, but it got the point across: RIDE WITH ME TO WINTER FORMAL!

With this latest turn in the race, Carolina and Patricia began to wonder whether the student body would support their efforts to have them both elected queen. But they didn't care. They had moved beyond that. Now what was important was raising—and showing—school spirit. And that they did. Well.

On Monday, they won the baby-picture contest. On Tuesday, they chewed huge wads of gum for the Can't Burst Our Bubble bubble gum competition. And by Saturday, the morning of winter formal, when they took to the football field to dance at the big game with the school mascot, the Groovin' Gator, the cousins both felt as though they hadn't had so much fun together in a really long time.

As they walked over to the stands, Carolina turned to her *prima* and said, "You know what, *chica*? I could care less about winning queen. I'm just relieved that you and I are tight again."

"Who you telling?" Patricia agreed. "I'm the one

who nearly crossed over to the shallow and superficial side with the SoBees."

"Hey, Patricia!" A guy with a deep voice yelled from behind her.

Turning around to see who was calling her, Patricia was shocked to discover that the voice was coming from the players' bench on the sideline. It was Jeff Giles, looking all kinds of wonderful in his C. G. High football uniform.

"What's up, Patty?" he yelled, waving before returning to the pregame huddle with his coach.

"What's down, Jeff?" Patricia nervously shouted back.

But Jeff was already in game mode and was now too focused to notice.

"He didn't hear you," Carolina giggled, squeezing her cousin's hand. "Which is a good thing, because you're a hot mess. 'What's down'? Really?"

Patricia was mortified. How was it possible that the sight of a cute guy could cause her to go from cool to corny in ten seconds flat?

Sensing that her *prima* was embarrassed, Carolina said, "Really, *chica*, do not sweat it. What matters is that in the midst of the most important game of the year, he noticed you, and he said hi."

"He called me Patty," Patricia swooned, as they took their seats among the hundreds of cheering football fans.

"Don't you hate that nickname?" Carolina asked.

"Oh, no," Patricia said as she sat down. "Jeff can call me Patty whenever he likes."

CHAPTER 16

LATER THAT NIGHT, hours before the big event, the New York Loft at The Setai twinkled with fairy lights. At the eleventh hour, a snow machine had been found in nearby Coconut Grove, and with the help of Maxo, Carmen had been able to rig the machine to a series of tracks above the room. (Of course, Carmen first had to get over her inability to speak coherently in front of him. But once she did, she discovered that Maxo wasn't just cute, he was *really* funny.) For the very first time in C. G. High history, the attendees at the dance would not just walk through snow on the ball-room floor. Snow would drift all around them, as if they had stepped into a snow globe.

It was still two hours before the formal began, but the drama was far from over. At the last minute, the SoBees had bowed out from the day's preparation, leaving everything in Carmen's hands.

"Now that Dorinda is running for queen, our priorities have shifted," Maya had explained.

"We have to support our queen," April had added.

Carmen had wanted to throw a fit. There were a gazillion things to do on the day of a big event, and it was totally uncool for the SoBees to bail just so they could spend the day at the salon getting ready. That said, even on their very best hardworking days, the efforts of Dorinda, April, and Maya didn't amount to much. They were always busy checking their e-mail, applying and reapplying their makeup, and making sure that whatever manner of mild manual labor they were engaged in had not damaged their hand commercial–worthy manicures.

They weren't worth it.

Plus, Carmen had a secret weapon. Ever since he'd helped her out with the snow-machine dilemma, Maxo had been Carmen's right-hand man. He was a technical genius and could fix *anything*. And with his help, C. G. High was about to have its greenest winter formal ever. It had been Maxo's idea that all the light fixtures in the ballroom be fitted with energy-saving bulbs. He had even found, at the last minute, an organic fruit and vegetable supplier who only purchased produce from local farms, and who was able to provide the caterer with food for a fraction of the price when the other caterer had pulled out.

Looking at him now, up in the rafters (where he looked really cute in his Moby T-shirt and work khakis), Carmen felt a little flutter. She'd been relieved to hear that Maxo and Carolina weren't an item, but she'd been too busy and a little too shy to act on it. Besides, there was something positively electric about crushing on a guy but not acting on it. Carmen was 99 percent sure that Maxo felt the same way. More than once, they'd been sitting side by side, going over budgets and spreadsheets for the formal, when she'd been sure that he'd been *this close* to kissing her, but he hadn't. She liked the idea that maybe he was a little shy, too. For now, the mystery was okay with her.

Carmen was putting the finishing touches on one of the food stations when Hillary Mantel, The Setai's events manager, walked in.

"Wow, I'm impressed," Hillary said, looking around the room.

"Thanks! We've been working so hard," Carmen replied. Like Maxo, she was dressed in work clothes. For Carmen, this meant an old T-shirt, olive green leggings, and her favorite Converse sneakers.

Hillary gestured up toward the rafters, where Maxo was adjusting the twinkling lights. "Your boyfriend's not too bad, either," she said softly.

Carmen flushed. "He's not my boyfriend," she said in a whisper.

"*Yet*," Hillary whispered back.

"Why do you say that?" Carmen asked, eager to get dating advice from the cool twentysomething woman.

Hillary smiled. "It's pretty obvious that he's not crazy about school dances. He's crazy about *you*."

Carmen smiled. "Now you sound like my *amigas*."

"Trust your *amigas*," Hillary said. "Mine have always had my back."

Carmen looked at her watch. Only two hours until the winter formal. "I was hoping to have enough time to go home, take a quick shower, and change. But it looks like that's not happening. No biggie. I brought my stuff. I can change in the bathroom here."

"No way," Hillary said. "Come with me."

Carmen looked up at the rafters, where Maxo was still working. "Are you okay, Maxo? I think I'm going to wrap things up and get changed."

"*Me suena bien*," he called out. "I'll see you at the dance. Save me one."

Hillary shook her head. "Utterly devoted and he

speaks Spanish, too? Repeat after me: *He's a keeper.* *He's a keeper.*"

Carmen laughed. "I know, the French is like the icing on the charming cake. But he's not mine to keep—"

"Yet," Hillary repeated.

Carmen followed her new friend to the elevators, wondering whether Hillary was offering to let her change in her office. But Hillary's office was on the second floor and she pressed the button for the fortieth floor, home of the Setai Spa. White billowy curtains made the giant reception area feel calm and intimate, and delicious-smelling aromatherapy candles filled the space with a soft yellow light. Women in white bathrobes and white and gold flip-flops walked across the room, several holding clear glass cups of tea. Carmen had been a complete and total ball of stress for months now. But even standing in the lobby of the spa was relaxing.

"You're going to let me change here?" Carmen asked.

"Isn't it wonderful?" Hillary mused.

They walked to the front desk, where a pretty woman in a sleeveless gold kimono top and a name tag that read MILLYS welcomed them.

"Miss Ramirez-Ruben is here for an important event tonight, Millys," Hillary said.

Carmen was thrilled to hear herself referred to in such a grown-up way.

"Absolutely," Millys replied. "I'll show you to our locker room and get you set up with a robe and slippers."

Hillary then said, "Once Miss Ramirez-Ruben is showered and dressed, please take her to see George and Dan."

Carmen was confused. "Who are George and Dan?"

"They're The Setai's top hair and makeup artists," Hillary explained.

"Oh, no—" Carmen began.

"Oh, yes," Hillary insisted. "And one final thing, Millys," she added. "Please make sure that Miss Ramirez-Ruben does not see a bill."

Although Carmen did her best to act professionally with adults, she couldn't help herself. She gave Hillary a huge hug. "Thank you, thank you, *un millón de gracias.*" She couldn't wait to tell Alicia and Jamie. They were going to *flip.*

Hillary hugged her back, clearly pleased at being able to give her new young friend such a big treat. "Think nothing of it. VIP treatment for a VIP client." Then she leaned over and whispered, "Besides, we C. G. High girls have to stick together."

As Hillary went back to her office, Carmen followed Millys into the locker room. Once there, Millys set her up with a locker and a robe. The minute the spa attendant was out of sight, Carmen whipped out her phone and began texting her girls: *Chilling at the spa at the setai. FYI, the locker room makes the cg high one look like a gas station toilet. LOL.*

Right away, Alicia wrote back: *You hanging with the SoBees now?*

Jamie replied: *Thanks for inviting me.*

Carmen explained the situation in quick texts. Then she headed over to one of the slate-tiled shower stalls and peeked in. The shower had four spa jets— two on each wall—and a giant rain-forest showerhead. She stepped in and proceeded to take the longest, most luxurious shower of her life.

Afterward, her hair still soaking wet, Carmen threw on her robe and, with her phone, took a picture of herself in the shower. She texted the picture to her sister Una, who spent hours pouring through photos of celebrity homes in magazines like *InStyle*.

But it was Maxo, not Una, who wrote back: *Um. Are you trying to tell me something?*

Carmen giggled and texted: *Oops! Sorry. Wrong number.*

Normally, she would have been embarrassed, but the same thing had happened to Jamie when she first met Dash. Maybe it was a sign that there was more to come for the two of them. Plus, she didn't have time for mental flip-out. She had to keep getting ready.

Millys had suggested that Carmen keep her robe on for hair and makeup, so she padded across the spa lobby to the salon. The room was filled with women her mother's age having their hair colored, shampooed, and styled. A receptionist led her to a chair in the corner, where she was greeted by two gorgeous men.

"Hi, I'm George. I do hair," said the redhead in the softly crinkled white linen shirt.

"And I'm Dan, I do faces," said the brunet in the yellow and green Brazilian soccer-team jersey.

"I'm Carmen," she said, reaching out to shake each of their hands. "And I do high school."

"So, sweetheart," George began, "you're young, you're gorgeous. We couldn't ask for better raw material. What we need to know is what the *story* is that you are telling tonight."

He sat down next to her and waited, as if preparing to hear a lecture on a very fascinating topic.

Carmen laughed. "Well, tonight's our school's winter formal. We're having it in the New York Loft upstairs, and I'm on the planning committee. I'm really into fashion, and I designed and made my own dress."

"A designer? How fabulous," George cooed. "We *must* see the dress."

Carmen stood up to go get it, but the men pushed her gently back into the chair.

"We have staff for that," George said, winking at Carmen.

Moments later, a spa attendant returned with Carmen's dress. It was a classic black minidress, sleeveless, made of Duchess satin. Except that Carmen had sewn a border of hot pink material around the hem.

"It was inspired by . . ." Carmen began.

"*The Devil Wears Prada*," George said, finishing her sentence. "It's stunning."

"It's fun," Dan said, approvingly. "I think we've got our story."

"Yes," George said, running a comb through Carmen's wet hair. "The look we're going for tonight is Park Avenue Princess."

An hour later, Carmen strode into the winter formal feeling every inch a princess. George had washed and styled her hair so that it fell in soft waves around her shoulders. He'd placed a few crystal pins in the back that caught the light and twinkled as she danced. Dan had modeled her makeup on that of the classic movie star, Audrey Hepburn, and her signature style in the movie *Breakfast at Tiffany's*. He explained, "Audrey's look was all about the three Bs: beautiful hair, big eyes, big smile." He'd even blended a special lip stain just for her, a pink that matched the pink on her dress perfectly. "I call this color Carmen in the City," Dan said, giving her a small tube of it and a very fancy lipstick brush that he let her keep.

Despite the star treatment, Carmen felt nervous as she walked through the ballroom. She knew she was being paranoid, but it felt like others kept stealing glances at her. She could have sworn she saw more than one girl point at her. Something was wrong. Was she trailing toilet paper on her shoe? She looked down. Nope. Her black satin pumps were fine. Was her skirt too short? She didn't think so. She looked around for her *amigas* and for Maxo, but she didn't see them anywhere.

It had been Carmen's idea to divide the room into four sections, representing different parts of New York City, with the dance floor in the middle. In the "downtown" section, there were high-top tables and metal bistro chairs. The food stations served classic New

York dishes: knishes and hot dogs to represent the Lower East Side, dim sum to represent Chinatown, and mini Cubano sandwiches to represent the Latin flavor of Greenwich Village eateries like Café Habana.

In the Jackson Heights "neighborhood," a big projector played a Bollywood film against one wall, and an Indian model handed out bindis, tiny jewels that were traditionally worn on the forehead, to all of the girls who wanted one. The food stations served popular Indian dishes like samosas, curries, and a nonalcoholic tamarind cocktail that Carmen had playfully dubbed The Slumdog Millionaire, after the popular film.

After making sure everything was going smoothly, Carmen went to find her friends. She found Jamie, Gaz, Dash, and Alicia hanging out in the Harlem section of the party. The boys were tearing into plates of fried chicken, and the girls were nibbling on mini crocks of mac and cheese.

"You look *amazing*," Alicia said, rising to give her friend a hug. Alicia was dressed in a Pucci print maxidress and gold hoop earrings. Her dark hair fell in perfect ringlets around her shoulders.

"The Spa Queen emerges," Jamie teased. Never one to go along with the crowd, Jamie was wearing a white turtleneck, a silver Burberry miniskirt, and a pair of black knee-high Gucci boots. She looked very mod and very cool.

Dash waved hello, and Gaz stood up to give Carmen a hug. "Domingo has no idea what he's missing," Gaz said.

Alicia slapped him on the shoulder. "Gaz! We don't mention that name."

"Mention what name?" Maxo asked, as he joined the group.

"Nobody," Alicia said, rolling her eyes at Gaz.

"It's okay," Carmen said. Then turning to Maxo, she gave him a once-over and smiled broadly. "You wash up nice."

Maxo smiled back. "A clean shirt and ironed pants do wonders. But you are a vision. All of you ladies are. The theme of this party should have been Angels and Mortals."

Dash whispered to Jamie, "Who is this guy? Does he talk like this all the time?"

She smiled and whispered back, "Pretty much."

"And do the girls really fall for all this Angels and Mortals talk?" Dash asked.

Jamie nodded and replied, "Pretty much."

The group was soon joined by Carolina and Patricia.

"Hey, you guys have to check out the Williamsburg

section," Patricia said. "They have brownies and an off-the-hook cherry ice-cream flavor called Brooklyn Bling Bing."

"Did somebody say, 'ice cream'?" Jeff Giles asked as he came by and joined the growing crowd. Judging by the way he looked at Patricia, it was clear that he was no longer on the fence about her. Clearly, she was way more than just a fellow jock to him now.

Patricia appraised her crush with a newly critical eye. If only he had been into her a little bit sooner. She wasn't so sure anymore that he was the one. After all, when the dance was over, she'd go back to being regular Patricia. And she liked her regular self and wanted the guy she was with to feel the same way. If she had learned anything from her fight with Carolina, it was that she had a lot to offer. And just because he made her swoon a little, it didn't mean he was the one. He'd have to prove himself to her now.

Jean-Luc had shown up and now stood next to Carolina. He gestured toward the dance floor. "I think something's happening," he said.

And sure enough, something was.

Standing in the middle of the dance floor, Dorinda— dressed in what everyone had to admit was a stunning red gown—was holding a microphone. "In just a few minutes, voting for the winter formal queen will end," she announced. "And while I speak to you in my capacity as head of the Socials and Benefits Committee, I'd be remiss if I didn't remind you that I'm also running for queen. Now, go vote!"

Standing at the side, Maya and April cheered her on.

Carmen raised a glass of fruit punch to Carolina and Patricia. "To you! May the best queens win!" All of the girls and their guys joined in the toast. Carolina and Patricia gave each other a confident high five.

Pulling Carmen aside, Maxo asked, "Do you like ice cream?"

"I love it," Carmen answered.

"Then let's go to Williamsburg," he said, offering her his hand as if it were the most natural thing in the world. And for once, Carmen didn't try to overanalyze. She just went with it.

They walked hand in hand over to the southern section of the ballroom. It featured a minipark area with park benches, real trees, and a Jamie Sosa mural of the Williamsburg Bridge. Carmen took a seat on the park bench while Maxo went to get ice cream.

He returned with two little cups of Brooklyn Bling Bing, and they sat side by side. Carmen looked around the room. Dash and Jamie, the best dancers she'd ever seen, were tearing up the dance floor. Gaz and Alicia were watching the Bollywood film in the Jackson Heights section. Everyone seemed to be enjoying the special effects and all the food. She'd planned many *quinces*, and she'd loved each and every one of them. But the winter formal was different. Thanks to the pure sloth of the SoBees, this was something that Carmen had imagined, and created, almost entirely on her own. As always, Jamie and Alicia had given her good advice, but she'd had to rely on her gut instincts—and that had felt good. When it came time next year to consider colleges, maybe it made sense not to limit her aspirations to just fashion design. Maybe there were other ways to be creative.

"Are you admiring your handiwork?" Maxo asked, after a few moments of comfortable silence.

Carmen nodded and smiled.

"You should be proud. This is like something out of a movie," Maxo said admiringly.

Carmen wanted to say, "Well, in a movie, this is the part where you'd kiss me." But instead, she said, "You were such a huge help, Maxo. I couldn't have done this without you."

He leaned forward, in that *I'm about to kiss you* way, and they were so much in their own world that

Carmen did not realize for a few moments that all eyes in the room were now on her. It only dawned on her when she heard Ms. Ingber, who was standing on the dance floor, microphone in hand, call Carmen's name.

"Carmen Ramirez-Ruben! Earth to Carmen! Would you please come up here?" Ms. Ingber bellowed into the mike.

Carmen's first impulse was panic. There was nothing in the schedule about her speaking. What did Ms. Ingber want? What was going on?

"Excuse me," she said, handing Maxo her ice cream. "I'll be right back."

She dashed over, wondering once again why everyone was staring at her. As if in slow motion, Ms. Ingber opened the velvet pouch that she held. Carefully, she took out a crystal-studded tiara and . . . placed it on Carmen's head.

"Ladies and gentlemen," Ms. Ingber announced. "Please join me in applauding this year's winter formal queen."

Carmen was in shock. "But I'm not even a candidate."

Ms. Ingber smiled. "I saw the ballots myself. You're not only a candidate, you're the *winning* candidate.

Congratulations. Now you have to pick some lucky guy as your king—and for your first dance."

Out of the corner of her eye, Carmen saw a furious Dorinda exiting the ballroom, followed by an equally annoyed Maya and April. She scanned the room and found Alicia, Jamie, Carolina, and Patricia jumping up and down and cheering in the SoHo section of the room.

"Excuse me, Ms. Ingber," Carmen said. "I'm going to need a few minutes before the dance."

At her teacher's nod, she rushed over to her girls. "What is going on?" she demanded. "Did I bump my head? Am I having one of those deluded, hospital-bed dreams?"

Carolina hooked arms with Carmen. "Last night, Patricia and I were talking. This quest for queen almost ruined our friendship."

"Spirit Week was so much fun; it was almost like running together was better than actually winning," Patricia added.

"So we began thinking about who should *really* be queen," Carolina continued.

"She had to be beautiful—inside and out," Patricia said. Gesturing all around the room, she added, "And it only seemed fair that the queen should be someone who worked her butt off on behalf of the entire school."

"So we started a write-in campaign," said Carolina, who held up her phone and showed Carmen a text that read: *Winter formal queen secret alert! write in your vote for Carmen Ramirez-Ruben; she's cool, she's kind, she's the heart of c. g. high. Text this to a friend (or 2, or 3 . . .)*

As Carmen stood staring at the text in disbelief, Hillary Mantel approached the group. "Congratulations, *chica*!" she exclaimed, giving her a huge hug.

Turning to face the *amigas*, Carolina, and Patricia, Hillary said, "That was one powerful text." She held up her phone. "It even made it to former C. G. High students."

Carmen's eyes widened. "That's why you hooked me up with George and Dan."

Hillary shook her head. "No, I hooked you up because you're awesome. But I secretly hoped that you'd be topping off their handiwork with a crown."

"You are the queen, *fíjate*," Alicia said. "Woo-hoo!"

"Speaking of which, aren't you supposed to be doing some kind of dance?" Jamie asked.

Maxo! In the madness of it all, Carmen had momentarily forgotten all about him.

She found him sitting just where she'd left him—on the park bench in Williamsburg.

"Your ice cream melted, so I threw it away," Maxo said, solemnly.

"I'm so sorry. I was, I still am, completely in shock. I wasn't even running for queen," Carmen explained.

"I know," Maxo said, holding up his phone to show the secret text. "I might have been the one who hacked into the C. G. High database and sent it to every student in the system. And I might have been the one who borrowed your phone this morning and deleted the text so you wouldn't see it."

"You did?" Carmen had been fighting back tears—though she wasn't sure that this was a fight she would win.

"I did," Maxo said, smiling.

"Well, then, I guess I owe you one. Will you dance with me?" Carmen asked.

"I will," he replied.

He led her out to the dance floor, and as they approached, all the couples who had been moving and grooving cleared the space.

Jamie ran over. "The DJ wants to know what song you want to dance to," she said.

Carmen didn't hesitate. "Moon River."

Jamie smiled and went to convey the queen's instructions.

"I don't know that song," Maxo said, as he placed one hand on her shoulder and one on her hip.

Carmen shivered a little at his touch, but confidently leaned in and pressed her cheek against his. "It's from *Breakfast at Tiffany's*, one of my favorite movies. I'll show it to you if you like."

"How about tomorrow? Could I come over tomorrow?" Maxo asked.

"Tomorrow is good," she replied, as the first notes of the song filled the room.

As they swayed to the music, she thought of George and Dan and their question: "What story do you want to tell tonight?" *Breakfast at Tiffany's* had been her inspiration. But she had been wrong. This story, this fairy tale, was completely her own. And it was completely wonderful.

CHAPTER 17

WHOEVER said that lightning doesn't strike twice had never encountered the awesome powers of Amigas Inc.

A week after the winter formal, it was time for Carolina and Patricia's joint *quince*. Carmen woke up, and, as she had done every day for the past week, she shook her hair out and put on her tiara. She only wore it while she brushed her teeth and ate breakfast. But the little silvery crown made her smile, and she felt bathed in the love of her best friends—Alicia and Jamie—as well as her new friends, Carolina and Patricia.

It was six a.m. on a Saturday morning, which meant that Carmen's household—loud and rambunctious a little later in the day—was silent and sleeping.

Carmen made herself a cup of café con leche and grabbed one of her mother's delicious currant scones from the basket near the fridge. Then she crept downstairs to the basement, where she had taken to keeping her sewing machine. On the garment rack near her work area were seven original Carmen Ramirez-Ruben original dresses. Two were white dresses for Carolina and Patricia's church ceremony; two others were formal dresses: one cream-colored with shades of pink, for Carolina, and the other also cream-colored, with shades of charcoal gray for Patricia. These dresses were for the party.

Three additional dresses were for her, Jamie, and Alicia. Since she hadn't had time to make them dresses for the winter formal, she'd surprise them with these. Each dress had a simple strapless bodice matched with a full skirt and a tulle slip underneath. As a bit of a joke, Carmen had designed the *amigas'* Mystery and Moonlight dresses as an homage to the SoBees' matching outfits. Alicia's dress was a silvery lavender. Jamie's dress was an emerald color that reminded Carmen of a putting green. Her own dress was canary yellow.

She placed each dress in the custom-monogrammed garment bags that her mother and Christian had made for her as Christmas presents. Each bag read AMIGAS INC. and, beneath that, ORIGINAL DESIGNS BY C. RAMIREZ-RUBEN.

Carmen took the dresses upstairs, showered, and

quickly changed into one of her mother's vintage Mexican dresses. It was white, thick cotton, with three-quarter-length sleeves and a hand-embroidered design in the center. It was the perfect Amigas Inc. work dress—appropriate enough for a church ceremony, but sturdy enough that you could do anything in it, from getting down on the floor to fix a ripped hem to pitching in and helping a particularly slow catering service. She put her hair in what she and her sister Una called a messy pretty updo. Then she looked in the mirror. *Cute*, she thought. On days when she was working hard on someone else's *quince*, "cute" was plenty good.

Carmen's mother, the designated driver, met her in the kitchen. She looked exhausted but pretty in a light blue tracksuit. "*Estoy cansada*," her mother said. "First stop, Starbucks."

Once they'd completed their coffee run, Carmen and her mother made the rounds like the *quince* equivalents of the tooth fairy. First, they stopped by Carolina's and left her dresses with the housekeeper.

"Señorita Carolina is still sleeping," the woman said cheerfully.

"Wake her up! It's her big day!" Carmen smiled, handing her a garment bag.

Next, they stopped at the other Reinoso household,

where they found Patricia and her father just back from a morning jog.

"Oooh, dresses!" Patricia called out as she ran up.

Carmen liked Patricia, but her jocklike ability to be perfectly sunny at seven in the morning was borderline alien.

"Here you go. See you at the church!" Carmen said, attempting to match Patricia's postjog energy with her own cheeriness.

Carmen next dropped off dresses for Alicia and Jamie. Finally, her mother dropped her off at the church.

"*Gracias* for all the early-morning chauffeuring," she said, giving her mother a hug and kiss.

"*De nada, hija,*" her mother said. "I'm very proud of you."

Carmen entered the church, admiring the space. More than a year of planning *quinces* had given her a greater appreciation of churches. Each was its own work of art. This particular sanctuary was beautiful: cathedral ceilings, dark oak woodwork, gold fixtures, and pale honey–colored walls. The candles were exactly where she'd placed them the night before. But the flowers—fragrant Casablanca lilies that were supposed to decorate the altars—were nowhere to be found. She checked the church office and discovered that even the bouquets for Carolina and Patricia had failed to arrive.

She quickly dialed the florist and looked at her watch. Two hours until the church ceremony, and this guy was a no-show. It happened occasionally—thankfully not often—that a vendor just completely slipped up. As she left unanswered message after unanswered message, Carmen soon began to realize that this was the case now.

She reached into her bag for her iPad and accessed the Google map application. There were five florists within a ten-mile radius of the church. She'd figure something out. She picked a shop called Florabunda, because she liked the name and because their Web site was cute, and dialed their number.

"Can you deliver two vases of Casablanca lilies in an hour?" she asked. "It's for a *quince* that's happening today, and our flowers didn't show up."

She listened as the woman on the phone quoted her an exorbitant fee.

"Uh-uh, too much," Carmen pushed back. "What else do you have? How about you do a mix of stargazers and Casablancas to keep the costs down? But no filler flowers and no carnations. Can you also make two hand bouquets? The bases need to be wrapped in satin.

"Those bouquets can be a mix of white and pink

roses," Carmen said. "Here's my cell, please call me if you have even the slightest question or problem."

She opened her purse and read the woman her credit card number. Reciting the sixteen digits never failed to make her feel grown-up. Alicia's mother had opened a corporate account in the name of Amigas Inc., and each girl had been issued a card in her own name. The rule was that they were to use the card only in emergencies—and, as Alicia's mother often reminded them—she meant *quince* emergencies, not I'm-at-the-mall-and-this-skirt-that's-on-sale-is-too-cute-not-to-buy emergencies.

Two hours later, the flowers had arrived, the guests had been seated, and the *quince* girls were standing at the altar in their new high heels. During the church ceremony, every *quinceañera* changed from flats to a pair of heels to symbolize her walk into womanhood.

Carmen sat in the second row of the church, next to Alicia and Jamie.

The minister approached the pulpit and gave his sermon. Afterward, he announced, "Our *quinceañeras* would like to address the congregation. First, we'll hear from Carolina Reinoso."

Carolina approached the microphone and smiled at

the churchgoers. "*Buenos días,* honored family, friends, and community members. I have been dreaming about a *quinceañera* since I was a little girl, and I am so blessed that my parents were able to give me one. I wanted to take a moment and share with you some thoughts on this day and the meaning of this celebration. What does a *quince* mean?

"The *q* in *quince* certainly stands for 'queen.' It's not that we are queens, but more that we are making a commitment to conduct ourselves in a manner that is beyond reproach. Patricia and I, like every *quinceañera,* are the daughters of queens. And we thank our mothers for their love and understanding.

"The *u* in *quince* stands for 'unity,'" she continued. "We stand before you, united in our family, united in our friendships, and united with the Latino community. The *i* in *quince,* at least for me and Patricia, stands for 'intrepid.' For us, life is an adventure, and we are so excited that this birthday marks the beginning of a new journey. The *n* in *quince* stands for '*no hay palabras.*' And there are literally no words to convey our gratitude for the role you all have played in making us the young women we are today. The *c* in *quince* stands for 'caring,' which we forgot to do for each other, but which we'll never forget again.

"And last, but not least, the *e* in *quince* stands for 'excellence.' And we promise you to strive for excellence in everything we do. Thank you."

The church erupted in applause, and the *amigas* exchanged knowing smiles. It would have been a shame, they all thought, if this amazing *quince* had been ruined because of the winter formal queen competition. Thank *Dios* that the Reinoso girls had worked their differences out.

Patricia took Carolina's place at the pulpit. "My cousin has spoken to you about the meaning of *quince* and what it symbolizes to us, and I just wanted to take a moment and add a few thoughts about the meaning of family. Everyone here knows that Carolina is not just my cousin. A cousin is someone you see at special occasions, who's related to you and familiar, someone you may or may not like, someone you may or may not love. A *prima hermana* is another matter entirely. We were born cousins, but we were raised as sisters. We know that that bond is rare, and we wanted to take a moment to salute our parents. Mama, Papa, please stand. *Tío*, *Tía*, please stand. It's because you all are so close that we have this gift of friendship and family today."

The parents of Carolina and Patricia stood up, and the entire congregation showered them with applause.

When the clapping finally died down, Patricia said a few more words, and then, almost as soon as it had started, the ceremony was over.

The *amigas* joined the other guests in a receiving line to greet the *quinces*. Standing in the sunlight on the patio of the church, they marveled at all that had happened and all that lay ahead.

"Well," Alicia said, "it's December. *Quince* season has officially begun."

The *amigas* knew that between Christmas and the end of the school year, there would be a flurry of parties. Some girls liked to have their *quinces* over the holidays, to take advantage of families' visiting town. Some girls waited months, to celebrate their fifteenth birthdays with a big New Year's Eve bash. Valentine's Day was a popular time for *quinces*, as was Easter. And in Miami in June, there were as many *quinces* as there were weddings.

"We're ready for it," Carmen said confidently.

"Carolina and Patricia are awesome," Jamie said, gesturing toward the girls who stood at the church door, looking beautiful in their white dresses.

"They're like honorary *amigas*," Alicia noted.

"I totally agree," Carmen said.

"You know who else is totally awesome? Maxo," Jamie said, playfully giving Carmen a little push.

Alicia grinned and clapped her hands. "Oh, my God. He's so into you."

Carmen just smiled.

"No, seriously," Alicia commented. "How does it feel to be worshipped like a goddess? I mean, a queen?"

Alicia was exaggerating only a bit. Maxo was a hopeless romantic, as Carmen was quickly learning. After their first winter formal dance, Maxo had fallen to one knee and kissed her hand; this had drawn praise and applause from all of the girls, but incredulous stares from the guys.

"He's just old-fashioned," Carmen said shyly.

Alicia raised an eyebrow. "Okay, fine. How does it feel to be worshipped like a goddess in an old-fashioned way?"

Carmen grinned. "You know what? It feels pretty great."

Jamie grew serious. "Can you believe that this time next year, we'll have applied to colleges?"

Alicia sighed. "I know. It's so wild. Time is flying by, and I have no idea what I'm going to do."

"Well, you know, I've got to get back to *Nueva* York by hook or by crook," Jamie said, enthusiastically. "Let's hope that Columbia University shows me some love. What about you, C.?"

Carmen smiled. "Me? I'm just enjoying all of the possibilities."

She'd always assumed that she'd apply to FIT or the Savannah College of Art and Design. But the past few weeks had changed everything. Hillary had studied hotel management at the Wharton School in Philadelphia, and that seemed exciting. Carmen had a cousin at the University of Texas in Austin; that school seemed interesting, too. And she loved everything she heard about the art program at Brown. More and more, it seemed that the best thing Carmen could do was to follow the advice Carolina and Patricia had given in their speech about *quinces*: be intrepid, and enjoy the adventure.

But all the talk about the future made the *amigas* wonder the same thing: what would happen to Amigas Inc. after they left for college?

"We need successors!" Alicia cried.

"I don't even *know* any freshmen," Carmen pointed out.

"Me, neither," Jamie added.

The group decided to start looking for a few good first-year students whom they could begin to train and to whom they could pass the *quince* business on to when they graduated—and they would do so, just as soon as they were finished wrapping up the Reinoso *quince*.

"Look at us," Jamie said. "Do you really think we're going to find three girls as fierce, flawless, and fabulous as us?"

Alicia admitted it was a tall order. "But Amigas Inc. is too special just to let it fade away when we're at college. We've got to pass it on to a great group of girls."

Carmen wasn't pressing the matter. "We'll find them! And remember, we've got our whole senior year to whip 'em into shape."

A Chat with Jennifer Lopez

When I first came up with the idea for the Amigas series, I thought about the many Latina women who, like Alicia, Jamie, and Carmen, had started out as entrepreneurial teenagers. Who, through hard work, imagination, and dedication, were able to take their passions and talents and become role models and successful adults. For me, Jennifer Lopez is such a woman. She has incredible drive and an amazing work ethic, qualities she shares with the girls in Amigas. They, too, needed an equal amount of determination to turn their quince-party-planning *business into a huge success.*

So, to get a better sense of this connection, I sat down with Jennifer, and we talked about quinces *and what it was like for her as a Latina girl growing up in New York City. Here are some more of her answers. . . .*

—J. Startz

1. When you were in high school, were you involved in any clubs or extracurricular activities? Did you play any sports? If so, what were they, and which one was your favorite?

I didn't play sports when I was in high school, but in elementary school, I ran track, did gymnastics, and played softball. I was the shortstop on our team in seventh grade and eighth grade! In high school, I was in our school's plays and musicals every year. I danced in all the musicals, and even choreographed some. I would have to say that was my favorite part of my extracurricular activities.

2. Did any of the activities that you were involved in as a high school student have an effect on your choice of career? If so, in what way?

While doing the shows in high school, I realized what hard work it was to be a performer. I learned how much work and commitment it took to put on a good show—every night, every time. Months and months of rehearsal have to go into it first, and then you have to perform at your peak the minute you hit the stage. So, while I already knew that I wanted to dance, act, and sing for a living, I realized that I needed the commitment, passion, and desire to do the hard work, to accomplish my dreams. So, I decided to do that!

3. Was prom or winter formal a big deal in your high school? What made going to a school formal in high school special for you?

Prom was a very big deal in my school. I went to an all-girls high school, so we looked forward to events where *boys would be around! I designed my own dress for the prom, too. It was pale pink satin, in a kind of mermaid shape. At the time, I loved it.*

4. The two *primas hermanas* have very different interests. Patricia is a super athlete and star basketball player. Carolina is more of an academic, and is very involved with Coral Gables' environmental club. Of the two cousins, whom do you feel most similar to?

I was definitely an athlete growing up, but I always worked on being a good student, too. I thought both were really important to focus on when I was a teenager.

5. Carmen gets drafted by her homeroom teacher to be on the planning committee for the winter formal and rises to the challenge of having to work with the SoBees, her school's version of "mean girls." When you were in high school, did you ever find yourself in this kind of uncomfortable social situation? How did you deal with it? What advice do you have for teens who feel they are being bullied or made to feel inferior by the popular "queen bee" clique in their school?

I think everyone at one time or another faces this kind of situation, and we all have to live through it. But the bullying topic always bothered me! It's become such an important issue lately, too. It is so important to remember to never treat anyone in a way that degrades them, or makes them feel bad about themselves. Also, if it's happening to you, remember that you do not have to keep quiet! Say something. Don't suffer in silence. No one should have to take harassment from anybody. Report it; tell parents and teachers. Make sure the adults in your life have a plan to deal with it. And know that no one is any better than you; just as you are not better or worse than anyone else. Everyone deserves to be treated kindly and with decency.

6. Patricia and Carolina both decide that they want to be voted as winter formal queen, and soon they are involved in a major competition. Have you ever been in a situation (personally or jobwise), in which you had to compete against a good friend for something you wanted very much? How did you feel about it, and how did you deal with it?

I always believe that the opportunities that are meant to be there for you come your way. I used to worry sometimes, when I was first starting out, Oh, I didn't win in that audition, I didn't get that one part I would really have liked. *But I realized later that you needn't worry about the competition, or what you are winning or not winning over somebody else. The things that are meant to be there for you will be there. You don't have to put any thought into any of the other stuff.*

Make sure to RSVP for the next quinceañera!

Amigas

Point Me to Tomorrow

by Veronica Chambers

Created by Jane Startz
Inspired by Jennifer Lopez

CHAPTER 1

ALICIA CRUZ couldn't remember the last time she'd had her friends over for a sleepover. They'd pretty much given up on them in the eighth grade. Which isn't to say they hadn't hung out all night long until the break of dawn ever since—not only in their hometown of Miami, but as far away as Spain. Sometimes they hung out for fun, like in the ninth grade, when for Alicia's fifteenth birthday, she had passed on the traditional Sweet Fifteen extravaganza, known the world over as a *quinceañera*, and instead traveled to Spain with her pal Carmen Ramirez-Ruben. In Barcelona, restaurants didn't even start serving dinner until nine, so Alicia and her parents and Carmen had dined many times at midnight and explored the Rambla, the heart of the city, as they strolled back to the hotel.

Two years ago, the late-night sessions had become more focused on work, when Alicia's desire to do a good deed and help a new girl in town plan her *quinceañera* turned into a full-blown business, Amigas Incorporated. And so, while Alicia had never had a *quince* of her own, she had now planned and attended dozens of them. She ran Amigas Inc. with Carmen and her other best friend and partner, Jamie Sosa. Now the three girls sat at the helm of the hottest teen-party-planning business in town—with a substantial company bank account and a very snazzy Young Entrepreneurs of Miami Award from the mayor's office to prove it.

Over the last couple of years, they'd spent many nights creating the most magical details for their clients. Alicia could hardly remember how many times she'd stayed up all night while Carmen, who was an ace seamstress and an amazing designer, put the finishing touches on a *quince* ball gown. They had all watched the sun rise from Jamie's studio, a garage turned working-artist's space, while Jamie completed a mural or a video project that took an already awesome celebration right over the top.

There wasn't anything you could tell Alicia and her girls about working hard. They'd all been there—blood, sweat, and tears—which was why Alicia wanted to have a sleepover. Lately, it seemed that every time they got together, it was a business meeting—everybody with their iPads out, diligently taking notes and penciling in dates. She missed having a simple girls' night in, with lots of good food, a cheesy DVD to laugh at, and nothing to do but relax and have a good time.

The doorbell rang, and Alicia knew it was Jamie, a dark-skinned Latina whose family originally came from the Dominican Republic. Having grown up in the Bronx, Jamie had been all hard edges and attitude. Then she fell in love with Dash Mortimer, the half Venezuelan, half American aristocrat and all-hottie golf player, and it rocked her world. Though it had taken a while for Jamie to reconcile the notion of herself as a girl from the streets with that of the girl who now hung out at country clubs and took private planes on the regular, the change had been good for her. Dash taught Jamie that she didn't have to be hard to be real.

Jamie now strutted into the Cruz family home in a slouchy charcoal cashmere sweater, leopard-print leggings, and sky-high heels. Alicia couldn't help laughing a little. "Come on, *chica*, I'm as fashion-forward as the next girl, but did you have to get so fancy for a sleepover?"

Jamie kicked her shoes off. "Ooooh, *Mami*, I just had an early dinner with Dash. He was in town for an

ESPN event last night, but he has to get back to Duke. I wanted to look cute—make sure I kept my edge over all those boy-crazy college girls."

In addition to crisscrossing the country on the junior PGA circuit, Dash Mortimer was a freshman at Duke University. Jamie had spent most of the summer trying to break up with him in anticipation of what she called "the inevitable," but Dash had finally convinced her that distance wasn't going to be their undoing. "It's over when it's over," he had told her one night after she picked another fight with him. Pulling her toward him for a kiss that seemed to last forever, he had said, "I don't know about you, but this doesn't feel like it's ever going to be over." It was only the last week of September, still early in the semester, and so far the unlikely couple was holding strong.

The doorbell rang again, and now Carmen joined them. Although she was the group's designated fashionista, she was dressed—as Alicia was—in sleepover-ready gear: an off-the-shoulder sweatshirt, black leggings, and neon pink fuzzy socks.

"Pajama party!" Carmen said, giving each of her friends the Latin *dobles* kiss—a peck on each cheek. Carmen was Chicana on her mother's side, Jewish Argentinean on her father's side, and as she liked to say, she wasn't half and half, she was one hundred percent Latina.

As the girls tucked in to a meal of takeout Indian— samosas, rice, and spicy chicken vindaloo—the conversation drifted to the big question mark on the horizon: college.

"So, Lici, is that T-shirt a sign of your coming around?" Jamie asked playfully. "All that ivy looks good on you."

Alicia was wearing a maroon and yellow Harvard T-shirt. Her parents had met at Harvard, and they'd made no secret of the fact that it would make them positively ecstatically happy if Alicia followed in their footsteps by attending that venerable institution.

Alicia blushed. "I just like wearing it, that's all."

Carmen tore off a piece of the Indian bread called naan and dipped it in the raita, a yogurt and cucumber dip that was the perfect cooling complement to the spicier dishes.

"And the fact that Gaz could be right down the road at Berklee doesn't have anything to do with it?" Carmen asked.

Berklee College of Music had one of the top programs in the country for aspiring musicians, and

Alicia's boyfriend and sometime *quince* collaborator, Gaz Colón, was a *serious* musician. He didn't just play in a high school garage band, he'd already signed a deal with an independent label in Nashville. They hadn't placed any of his tunes yet, but Alicia had no doubt that one of Gaz's sweet and sexy love songs would have audiences cheering in the rafters and would be playing on a million iPods sooner or later.

She loved him. She adored his music. She just wasn't sure how much she should let her relationship influence what felt like the most important decision of her life.

"I don't know," Alicia replied, feeling uncharacteristically nervous and uncertain. "Don't you guys think it's lame to choose a school based on where your boyfriend is going to college?"

Jamie held up one finger and gave Alicia a little South Bronx head swivel. "Oh, come on, *chica*. When that school is Harvard, the most prestigious university in da world, the answer is no, it's not lame."

"But it's where my parents went. It's where my boyfriend wants me to go. There's no *me* in that equation." Alicia rested her head on Carmen's shoulder. "You understand, right, C.?"

Carmen patted her friend's arm reassuringly, just

the way she had when Alicia had gotten food poisoning the time they all went to Key West to plan a *quince* for a very eccentric girl who lived in a house full of three-legged cats.

"Alicia," Carmen replied, "you're large and in charge. It's not what you choose to do, it's who you are. And you'll be running the joint, with a pile of friends and fans, wherever you go."

Alicia looked reassured; she always was when Carmen gave her advice. It wasn't just that Carmen was her oldest friend—which she was—it was also that Carmen had the mellow vibe of a Zen yoga master.

"Thanks, C.," Alicia said. "What about you guys? Things all moving along according to plan?"

"I'm trying to keep it simple," Jamie answered. "I'm planning to apply to three colleges in my favorite city, which, of course, is NYC. To mix things up a bit, I'm also looking at two schools with great graphic-design departments: Savannah College of Art and Design, and there's a dual program at Brown and Rhode Island School of Design."

"I'm going to apply to twelve colleges," Carmen said, smiling, "which seems like eight too many, but when your mom teaches high school, going above and beyond is the name of the game. Then we'll see where

I get in and what I can afford. My dad's latest *telenovela*, *¡Qué Lástima!*, just went into syndication in twenty-two countries, so *Papá* says if I get into almost anywhere, he'll cover the tuition, so I should be okay."

"What about 'To the Max' Maxo?" Jamie said. "Boyfriend have any preferences?"

Maxo was Carmen's new "guyfriend," as she called him. They'd hooked up at the end of junior year. Alicia and Jamie liked to call him "To the Max" Maxo, because he was cute—to the max; smart—to the max; and sweet—well, to the max.

Carmen smiled. "Maxo is actually going to take a year off to work with the Geekcorps in Haiti. He's going to be part of a volunteer IT team that helps local communities become more proficient in information and communications technologies."

"See?" Jamie laughed. "He's even a do-gooder—to the max."

"And you'll be okay with him being in another country for a whole year?" Alicia wondered.

Carmen shrugged, "Are you kidding? The rebuilding effort down there will take *years*, if not decades. I'm so proud of him for being willing to sacrifice a year to make a difference. I'll miss him, just like I'll miss you guys. But I want everyone I love to follow their dreams, no matter where they take them."

"You're awesome, Carm. I wish I could be as relaxed and mature as you are about this senior-year decision-making stuff," Alicia said as she put down her fork. "What I love about *quinceañeras* is that they are all about ritual and transition. You turn fifteen. You go to a church and the priest blesses you. You change from flat shoes to high heels. Presto change-o, you're no longer a kid, you're a woman. Then you have a big party and you dance the night away. Why can't finishing high school be like that?"

Jamie and Carmen both raised their eyebrows. Alicia very rarely had meltdowns. But when she did, they tended to be epic—and the girls had a feeling that deep in their friend's heart, a meltdown of legendary proportions was brewing.

"Sweetie," Carmen offered, "there's a process for finishing high school. It's called graduation."

Jamie reached for Alicia's *quince* crown and added, "You even get to wear a funny hat. There are speeches and a formal ceremony, just like in a *quince*. And there are huge parties after."

Alicia did not look satisfied. "But that comes when all the hard work is done, when you've taken your SATs, applied to colleges, and actually decided where you want to go. The difficult part is now, when there's a million decisions to make and each one feels way significant." Biting the straw in her drink, she said, "You know what I wish?"

Jamie shook her head. "I have no idea."

Carmen shrugged. "Not a clue."

"I wish there were an equivalent of us, an Amigas Inc., to guide you through the whole process—from college tours to SATs to applications and decision making."

Jamie reached into her purse for a tube of lip gloss. "Uh, *duh*. There is. It's called guidance counselors."

Alicia shook her head. "See, that's like saying regular party-planners are like us. If only there were girls who'd just been through it, who could help you decide."

Carmen knew then that her friend was really scared, not just about whether or not she'd go to Harvard, but about all the other changes that lay ahead, too. "Lici," she said tenderly, "*no te preocupes*. We'll help each other through this. We'll do what we always do when we plan a *quince*. We'll make a checklist. We'll divide the tasks according to our strengths, and we'll rock it out. Just like we always do."

"Pinkie promise?" Alicia said, extending a little finger to each of her best friends.

The girls locked fingers.

"There's only one thing that could make me feel even better," Alicia said shyly.

"And what's that?" Carmen asked, glad that her friend seemed to have been talked down from the ledge.

"If Jamie would lend me her mad hot shoes. They are fabulous, and they are *spanking new*. Not like mine, which are cute, but hand-me-downs from my mom." Alicia slipped the shoes on and ran out into the hall. She was quite a sight in her worn-out Harvard T, navy cutoffs, and runway-ready patent-leather heels.

"I got those shoes on eBay," Jamie said, running after her.

"Of course you did," Alicia grinned. Jamie's prowess at finding incredible deals online was legendary.

"They come from a seller in Antwerp," Jamie added as she caught up to Alicia. "That style never even came to the US."

Alicia took the shoes off and tossed one to Carmen. "Feel that leather, Carmen. It's like *buttah*," she laughed.

Jamie stood between Alicia and Carmen, desperately trying to catch one of her shoes as they sailed over her head. "You do know that you're playing hot potato with a very exquisite pair of heels, don't you?" she asked.

"And to think," Alicia said innocently, "back in the eighth grade, we played hot potato with real potatoes. What a bore!" Then she dissolved in giggles, relieved that, although as seniors in high school they were too old for many things, sleepovers weren't among them.

CHAPTER 2

THE NEXT MORNING, Alicia and her friends gathered at the snack bar of the quad outside their school, Coral Gables High. C. G. High was located in one of Miami's most luxurious residential neighborhoods. Even though September in Miami was plenty warm, the girls had shifted from their summer uniforms of strapless dresses, flip-flops, and sandals into the long cardigans, leggings, and knee-high boots that signaled the onset of fall and the beginning of the school year.

As they sipped various drinks, they were greeted by students they barely knew. They smiled and waved hello, feeling sometimes a little like reality TV stars. Like it or not, if you build a business throwing the hottest *quinceañeras* in town, you're more than just popular, you're kinda famous.

Rafael, a cute and incredibly built guy who was

captain of the swimming team, called out to them, "Hey, *chicas*, when's the next bangin' birthday party?"

Jamie smiled sweetly and said, "Wow, I wish I could tell you, but that's not how this works. You actually have to be invited by the birthday girl to the party."

Rafael grinned. "See, that's why y'all need to open up a club or something."

Jamie laughed, "A club? Um, we're just trying to get into college."

"I hear that," Rafael agreed, holding up his hand for a high five. Jamie gave him some dap, and before he walked away, he said, "Have a nice day, ladies. Try to slip me an invite for your next shindig."

As they watched him leave, Carmen said, "Remember when we were freshmen? We would have just *melted* if a guy like Rafael ever talked to us."

Jamie agreed. "Now we've all got boyfriends."

Carmen nodded. "Really awesome boyfriends."

"And we've got our own business," Alicia added proudly.

"It's incredible." Carmen looked a little dumbfounded. "I feel so lucky."

Jamie disagreed. "Not me," she told her friends. "Luck had nothing to do with it. We've worked really hard to be this successful."

Alicia looked at her friend admiringly. As confident as she felt herself to be, Jamie was even more so. Part of the fun of being Jamie's friend was trying to channel some of her bravado.

"Speaking of successful, I received a very interesting e-mail yesterday." Alicia pointed to her iPad.

"Let me guess," Jamie said. "Someone wants us to plan their *quince.*"

Alicia took a seat at the high-topped table and fanned her drink to cool it off. She took a packet of sugar out of her army-navy-style hobo purse.

Carmen laughed. "You know who else keeps sugar in her purse? My seventy-year-old grandmother from Argentina."

Alicia smiled and said, "That's because your *abuela* is very, very wise. Don't hate, appreciate."

Jamie pointed to the iPad and said, "So, the next client—who is it?"

They had planned *quinces* for girls from every imaginable background—from *Boricuas* to *Baranquilleras.* They had planned a space-themed *quince*, a *quince* on a yacht, and even a goth Latina *quince* on a cattle ranch in Texas. And they did their best to throw unforgettable parties—regardless of the client's budget. Big paychecks were nice, but they all agreed that their "under a thousand" *quinces* were some of the best parties they'd ever thrown.

"It's quite mysterious, actually," Alicia said. "Check this out." And she showed them the e-mail.

Dear Amigas Inc.,

It is with great delight that I write you on behalf of my client, a young woman of some renown—who, along with her parents, would like to enlist your services to plan what we hope will be a simply extraordinary *quince*.

The date we have in mind is Saturday, December 15. It is necessary to maintain a mystery about this event, at my client's request.

If you are available to take on this assignment, then all details will be managed via e-mail by me, the client's personal secretary.

Cordialmente,
Julia Centavo

Jamie looked at the dozens of students making their way across the campus. "Clearly, this is a joke," she remarked. "Someone is just having a laugh."

Alicia shook her head. "That was my first thought, too. Which is why I wrote back right away."

She read them her reply.

Dear Miss Centavo,

We appreciate your interest. But we are busy
students and entrepreneurs. We simply don't have
the time to pursue a "mystery *quince*."

Sinceramente,
Alicia Cruz

"Okay, so the prank is dealt with. Conversation
over, right?" said Carmen.

Alicia shook her head, tapped her iPad, and pulled
up another e-mail.

Dear Ms. Cruz,

Of course, your time is valuable. And as such, and
in consideration of the logistical complications of
keeping this client's identity a secret, we'd like to
offer you a two hundred dollar signing bonus, which
we have taken the liberty of wiring to your account.

Hasta pronto,
Julia Centavo

"This is starting to freak me out a little bit," Carmen
said. "Doesn't it all seem a little Da Vinci Code to you?"

"Forget about conspiracy fiction," Jamie jumped in, cutting to the chase. "First, check our account to see if the money is there."

Alicia pulled up their bank's home page and tapped in the user name and password. She took a deep breath, then turned the screen so her friends could see.

"Two hundred dollars. Deposited at nine this morning," Alicia noted.

"Who's the deposit from?" Carmen asked.

Alicia pulled up the details of the deposit and read: "SAP LLC."

"What's that?" Carmen wondered out loud.

"Who cares?" Jamie said. "Their money is good, I'm in."

"I don't know," Carmen countered. "I like to know who I'm working for. It could be someone shady."

Alicia nodded. "I agree; let's do some investigating. I'm going to try to find out who Julia Centavo is. Carmen, why don't you look into this SAP LLC? Jamie, can you do some online research on all the celebrities who might be celebrating *quinces* in Miami over the next six to eight months?"

To be continued . . .